The Point of View

Elinor Glyn

CHAPTER I

The restaurant of the Grand Hotel in Rome was filling up. People were dining rather late—it was the end of May and the entertainments were lessening, so they could dawdle over their repasts and smoke their cigarettes in peace.

Stella Rawson came in with her uncle and aunt, Canon and the Honorable Mrs. Ebley, and they took their seats in a secluded corner. They looked a little out of place—and felt it—amid this more or less gay company. But the drains of the Grand Hotel were known to be beyond question, and, coming to Rome so late in the season, the Reverend Canon Ebley felt it was wiser to risk the contamination of the over-worldly-minded than a possible attack of typhoid fever. The belief in a divine protection did not give him or his lady wife that serenity it might have done, and they traveled fearfully, taking with them their own jaeger sheets among other precautions.

They realized they must put up with the restaurant for meals, but at least the women folk should not pander to the customs of the place and wear evening dress. Their subdued black gowns were fastened to the throat. Stella Rawson felt absolutely excited—she was twenty-one years old, but this was the first time she had ever dined in a fashionable restaurant, and it almost seemed like something deliciously wrong.

Life in the Cathedral Close where they lived in England was not highly exhilarating, and when its duties were over it contained only mild gossip and endless tea-parties and garden-parties by way of recreation.

Canon and the Honorable Mrs. Ebley were fairly rich people. The Uncle Erasmus' call to the church had been answered from inclination—not necessity. His heart was in his work. He was a good man and did his duty according to the width of the lights in which he had been brought up.

Mrs. Ebley did more than her duty—and had often too much momentum, which now and then upset other people's apple carts.

She had, in fact, been the moving spirit in the bringing about of her niece Stella's engagement to the Bishop's junior chaplain, a young gentleman of aesthetic aspirations and eight hundred a year of his own.

Stella herself had never been enthusiastic about the affair. As a man, Eustace Medlicott said absolutely nothing at all to her— though to be sure she was quite unaware that he was inadequate in this respect. No man had meant anything different up to this period of her life. She had seen so few of them she was no judge.

Eustace Medlicott had higher collars than the other curates, and intoned in a wonderfully melodious voice in the cathedral. And quite a number of the young ladies of Exminster, including the Bishop's second daughter, had been setting their caps at him from the moment of his arrival, so that when, by the maneuvers of Aunt Caroline Ebley, Stella found him proposing to her, she somehow allowed herself to murmur some sort of consent.

Then it seemed quite stimulating to have a ring and to be congratulated upon being engaged. And the few weeks that followed while the thing was fresh and new had passed quite pleasantly. It was only when about a month had gone by that a gradual and growing weariness seemed to be falling upon her.

To be the wife of an aesthetic high church curate, who fasted severely during Lent and had rigid views upon most subjects, began to grow into a picture which held out less and less charm for her.

But Aunt Caroline was firm—and the habit of twenty-one years of obedience held.

Perhaps Fate was looking on in sympathy with her unrest. In any case, it appeared like the jade's hand and not chance which made Uncle Erasmus decide to take his holiday early in the year and to decide to spend it abroad—not in Scotland or Wales as was his custom.

Stella, he said, should see the eternal city and Florence before settling down in the autumn to her new existence.

Miss Rawson actually jumped with joy—and the knowledge that Eustace Medlicott would be unable to accompany them, but might join them later on, did not damp her enthusiasm.

The Point of View

Every bit of the journey was a pleasure, from the moment they landed on French soil. They had come straight through to Rome from Paris, where they had spent a week at a small hotel; because of the lateness of the year they must get to their southern point first of all and return northward in a more leisurely manner.

And now anyone who is reading this story can picture this respectable English family and understand their status and antecedents, so we can very well get back to them seated in the agreeable restaurant of the Grand Hotel at Rome—beginning to partake of a modest dinner.

Mrs. Ebley (I had almost written the Reverend Mrs. Ebley!) was secretly enjoying herself—she had that feeling that she was in a place where she ought not to be—through no fault of her own—and so was free to make the most of it, and certainly these well- dressed people were very interesting to glance at between mouthfuls of a particularly well-cooked fish.

Stella was thrilling all over and her soft brown eyes were sparkling and her dazzlingly pink and white complexion glowing with health and excitement, so that even in the Exminster confection of black grenadine she was an agreeable morsel for the male eye to dwell upon.

There were the usual company there: the younger diplomats from the Embassies; a sprinkling of trim Italian officers in their pretty uniforms; French and Austrian ladies; as well as the attractive-looking native and American representatives of the elite of Roman society.

The tables began to fill up before the Ebleys had finished their fish, and numbers of the parties seemed to know one another and nod and exchange words en passant.

But there was one table laid for a single person which remained empty until the entrees were being handed, and Stella, with her fresh interest in the whole scene, wondered for whom it was reserved.

He came in presently—and he really merits a descriptive paragraph all to himself.

He was a very tall man and well made, with broad shoulders and a small head. His evening clothes, though beautifully pressed, with that look which only a thoroughly good valet knows how to stamp upon his master's habiliments as a daily occurrence, were of foreign cut and hand, and his shirt, unstarched, was of the finest pleated cambric.

These trifles, however, were not what rendered him remarkable, but that his light brown hair was worn parted in the middle and waved back a la vierge with a rather saintly expression, and was apparently just cut off in a straight line at the back. This was quite peculiar-looking enough—and in conjunction with a young, silky beard, trimmed into a sharp point with the look of an archaic Greek statue, he presented a type not easily forgotten. The features were regular and his eyes were singularly calm and wise and blue.

It seemed incredible that such an almost grotesque arrangement of coiffure should adorn the head of a man in modern evening dress. It should have been on some Byzantine saint. However, there he was, and entirely unconcerned at the effect he was producing.

The waiters, who probably knew his name and station, precipitated themselves forward to serve him, and with leisurely mien he ordered a recherche dinner and a pint of champagne.

Stella Rawson was much interested and so were her uncle and aunt.

"What a very strange-looking person, " Mrs. Ebley said. "Of what nation can he be? Erasmus, have you observed him? "

Canon Ebley put on his pince-nez and gave the newcomer the benefit of a keen scrutiny.

"I could not say with certainty, my dear. A northerner evidently— but whether Swedish or Danish it would be difficult to determine, " he announced.

"He does not appear to know he is funny-looking, " Stella Rawson said, timidly. "Do you notice, Aunt Caroline, he does not look about him at all, he has never glanced in any direction; it is as if he were alone in the room. "

"A very proper behavior, " the Aunt Caroline replied severely, "but he cannot be an Englishman—no Englishman would enter a public place, having made himself remarkable like that, and then be able to sit there unaware of it; I am glad to say our young men have some sense of convention. You cannot imagine Eustace Medlicott perfectly indifferent to the remarks he would provoke if he were tricked out so. "

Stella felt a sudden sympathy for the foreigner. She had heard so ceaselessly of her fiance's perfections!

"Perhaps they wear the hair like that in his country, " she returned, with as much spirit as she dared to show. "And he may think we all look funny, as we think he does. Only he seems to be much better mannered than we are, because he is quite sure of himself and quite unconscious or indifferent about our opinion. "

Both her aunt and uncle looked at her with slightly shocked surprise—and she saw it at once and reddened a little.

But this incident caused the remarkable looking foreigner to crystallize in interest for her, especially when, in raising his glass of champagne, she saw that on his wrist there was a bracelet of platinum with a small watch set with very fine diamonds. She could hardly have been more surprised if he had worn a ring in his nose, so unaccustomed was she to any type but that of the curates and young gentlemen of Exminster.

Canon and Mrs. Ebley finished their dinner in disdainful silence and sailed from the room with chilling glances, but as Stella Rawson followed them demurely she raised her soft eyes when she came to the object of her relatives' contempt, and met his serene blue ones— and for some reason thrilled wildly.

There was a remarkable and powerful magnetism in his glance; it was as if a breath of some other world touched her, she seemed to see into possibilities she had never dreamed about. She resented being drawn into a far corner on the right hand of the hall, and there handed an English paper to read for half an hour before being told to go to bed. She was perfectly conscious that she was longing for the stranger to come out of the restaurant, that she might see him again.

But it was not until she was obediently following her aunt's black broche train to the lift up the steps again that the tall man passed them in the corridor. He never even glanced in their direction, and went on as though the space were untenanted—but had hardly got beyond, when he turned suddenly, and walked rapidly to the lift door, passing them again. So that the four entered it presently, and were taken up together.

Stella Rawson was very close to the remarkable looking creature. And again a wild nameless attraction crept over her. She noticed his skin was faintly browned with the sun, but was otherwise as fine as a child's—finer than most children's. And now she could see that three most wonderful pearls were his shirt-studs.

He got out on the second floor, one beneath them, and said, "Pardon, " as he passed, but not as a French word, nor yet as if it were English.

During these few seconds Stella was quite aware that he had never apparently looked at her.

"I call such an appearance sacrilegious, " Mrs. Ebley said. "A man has no right to imitate one of the blessed apostles in these modern days; it is very bad taste. "

CHAPTER II

Stella Rawson woke the next day with some sense of rebellion. There came with the rest of her post a letter from her betrothed. And although it was just such a letter as any nice girl engaged of her own free will to the Bishop's junior chaplain ought to have been glad to receive, Stella found herself pouting and criticizing every sentence.

"I do wish Eustace would not talk such cant, " she said to herself. "Even in this he is unable to be natural—and I am sure I shall not feel a thing like he describes when I stand in St. Peter's. I believe I would rather go into the Pantheon. I seem to be tired of everything I ought to like to-day! " And still rebellious she got up and was taken by her uncle and aunt to the Vatican—and was allowed to linger only in the parts which interested them.

"I never have had a taste for sculpture, " Mrs. Ebley said. "People may call it what names they please, but I consider it immoral and indecent. "

"A wonder to me, " the Uncle Erasmus joined in, "that a prelate— even a prelate of Rome—should have countenanced the housing of all these unclothed marbles in his own private palace. "

Stella Rawson stopped for a second in front of an archaic Apollo of no great merit—because it reminded her of the unknown; and she wished with all her might something new and swift and rushing might come into her humdrum life.

After luncheon, for which they returned to the hotel, she wearily went over to the writing-table in the corner of the hall to answer her lover's chaste effusion—and saw that the low armchair beside the escritoire was tenanted by a pair of long legs with singularly fine silk socks showing upon singularly fine ankles—and a pair of strong slender hands held a newspaper in front of the rest of the body, concealing it all and the face. It was the English TIMES, which, as everybody knows, could hide Gargantua himself.

She began her letter—and not a rustle disturbed her peace.

"Dearest Eustace, " she had written, "we have arrived in Rome—" and then she stopped, and fixed her eyes blankly upon the column of

7

births, marriages, and deaths. She was staring at it with sightless eyes, when the paper was slowly lowered and over its top the blue orbs of the stranger looked into hers.

Her pretty color became the hue of a bright pink rose. "Mademoiselle, " a very deep voice said in English, "is not this world full of bores and tiresome duties; have you the courage to defy them all for a few minutes—and talk to me instead? "

"Monsieur! " Miss Rawson burst out, and half rose from her seat. Then she sat down again—the unknown had not stirred a muscle.

"Good, " he murmured. "One has to be courageous to do what is unconventional, even if it is not wrong. I am not desirous of hurting or insulting you—I felt we might have something to say to each other—is it so—tell me, am I right? "

"I do not know, " whispered Stella lamely. She was so taken aback at the preposterous fact that a stranger should have addressed her at all, even in a manner of indifference and respect, that she knew not what to do.

"I observed you last night, " he went on. "I am accustomed to judge of character rapidly—it is a habit I have acquired during my travels in foreign lands—when I cannot use the standard of my own. You are weary of a number of things, and you do not know anything at all about life, and you are hedged round with those who will see that you never learn its meaning. Tell me—what do you think of Rome—it contains things and aspects which afford food for reflection, is it not so? "

"We have only been to the Vatican as yet, " Stella answered timidly—she was still much perturbed at the whole incident, but now that she had begun she determined she might as well be hung for a sheep as a lamb, and she was conscious that there was a strong attraction in the mild blue eyes of the stranger. His manner had a complete repose and absence of self-consciousness, which usually is only to be found in the people of race—in any nation.

"You were taken to the Sistine Chapel, of course, " he went on, "and to the loggia and Bramant's staircase? You saw some statues, too, perhaps? "

"My uncle and aunt do not care much for sculpture, " Miss Rawson said, now regaining her composure, "but I like it—even better than pictures. "

The stranger kept his steady eyes fixed upon her face all the time.

"I have a nymph in my house at home, " he returned. "She came originally from Rome; she is not Greek and she is very like you, the same droop of head—I remarked it immediately—I am superstitious—I suppose you would call what I mean by that word— and I knew directly that some day you, too, would mean things to me. That is why I spoke—do you feel it, too? "

Stella Rawson quivered. The incredible situation paralyzed her. She—the Aunt Caroline's niece, and engaged to Eustace Medlicott, the Bishop's junior chaplain, to be listening to a grotesque- looking foreigner making subtle speeches of an insinuating character, and, far from feeling scandalized and repulsed, to be conscious that she was thrilled and interested—it was hardly to be believed!

"Will you tell me from where you come? " she asked with sweet bashfulness, raising two eyes as soft as brown velvet. "You speak English so very well—one cannot guess. "

"I am a Russian, " he said simply. "I come from near Moscow—and my name is Sasha Roumovski, Count Roumovski. Yours, I am aware, is Rawson, but I would like to know how you are called— Mary, perhaps? That is English. "

"No, my name is not Mary, " she answered, and froze a little—but the Russian's eyes continued to gaze at her with the same mild frankness which disarmed any resentment. She felt they were as calm as deep pools of blue water—they filled her with a sense of confidence and security—which she could not account for in any way.

Her color deepened—something in his peaceful expectancy seemed to compel her to answer his late question.

"My Christian name is Stella, " she said, rather quickly, then added nervously: "I am engaged to Mr. Eustace Medlicott, an English clergyman—we are going to be married in September next. "

"And this is May, " was all Count Roumovski replied; then, for the first time since he had addressed her, he turned his eyes from her face, while the faintest smile played round his well-cut mouth.

"A number of things can happen in four months. Are you looking forward to your life as the wife of a priest—but I understand it is different in England to in my country—there I could not recommend the situation to you. "

Stella found absolutely no answer to this. She only felt a sudden, wild longing to cry out that the idea of being a curate's wife— even the Bishop's junior young gentleman with eight hundred a year of his own—had never appeared a thrilling picture, and was now causing her a feeling of loathing. She thought she ought to talk no longer to this stranger, and half rose from her seat.

He put out a protesting hand, both had been clasped idly over the Times until then without a movement.

"No—do—not go—I have disturbed you—I am sorry, " he pleaded. "Listen, there is a great reception at your Embassy to-morrow night—for one of our Royal Family who is here. You will go, perhaps. If so, I will do so also, although I dislike parties—and there I will be presented to you with ceremony—it will appease that English convention in you, and after that I shall say to you a number of things—but I prefer to sit here and speak behind the Times. "

At this instant he raised the paper, and appeared again the stranger almost entirely hidden from view. And Stella saw that her Uncle Erasmus was rapidly approaching her with an envelope in his hand. She seized her pen again and continued her broken sentence to Eustace—her betrothed. Canon Ebley viewed the Times and its holder with suspicion for an instant, but its stillness reassured him, and he addressed his niece.

"Very civil of the Embassy to send us a card for the reception to-morrow night, Stella; I am glad we wrote names when we arrived. Your Aunt Caroline bids you accept, as her spectacles are upstairs. "

Miss Rawson did as she was bid, and her uncle waited, fidgeting with his feet. He wished the stranger to put down the Times, which he wanted himself—or, at all events, remove his long legs and hidden body from such a near proximity to his niece; they could not say a word that he could not overhear, Canon Ebley mused.

However, the unknown remained where he was, and turned a page of the paper with great deliberation.

"Your aunt will be ready to go out again now, " the Uncle Erasmus announced, as Stella placed her acceptance in the envelope. "You had better go up and put your hat on, my dear. "

The Times rustled slightly—and Stella replied a little hurriedly: "I was just finishing a letter, uncle, then I will come. "

"Very well, " said Canon Ebley, not altogether pleased, as he walked away with the note.

The newspaper was lowered a few inches again, and the wise blue eyes beneath the saintly parted hair twinkled with irresistible laughter, and the deep voice said:

"He would greatly disapprove of our having conversed—the uncle— is it not so? How long are you going to stay in Rome? "

Stella smiled, too—she could not help it.

"A week—ten days, perhaps, " she answered, and then rapidly addressed an envelope to the Rev. Eustace Medlicott.

"Perhaps, in that case, I can afford to wait until to-morrow night; unless it amuses you, as it does me, to circumvent people, " Count Roumovski said. "We are all masters of our own lives, you know, once we have ceased to be children—it is only convention which persuades us to submit to others' authority. "

Stella looked up startled. Was this indeed true? And was it simply convention which had forced her into an engagement with Eustace Medlicott, and now forced her to go up and put on her hat and accompany her uncle and aunt to see the Lateran, when she would have preferred to remain where she was and discuss abstract matters with this remarkable stranger.

"The notion surprises you, one sees, " Count Roumovski went on, "but it is true—"

11

"I suppose it is, " said Stella lamely.

"I submit to no authority—I mean, as to the controlling of my actions and wishes. We must all submit to the laws of our country, to do so is the only way to obtain complete personal freedom. "

"That sounds like a paradox, " said Stella.

"I have just been thinking, " he went on, without noticing the interruption, "it would be most agreeable to take a drive in my automobile late this after-noon, when your guardians have returned and are resting. If you feel you would care to come I will wait in this hall from five to six. You need not take the least notice of me, you can walk past, out of the hotel, then turn to the left, and there in the square, where there are a few trees, you will see a large blue motor waiting. You will get straight in, and I will come and join you. Not anyone will see or notice you—because of the trees, one cannot observe from the windows. My chauffeur will be prepared, and I will return you safely to the same place in an hour. "

Stella's brown eyes grew larger and larger. Some magnetic spell seemed to be dominating her, the idea was preposterous, and yet to agree to it was the strongest temptation she had ever had in all her life. She was filled with a wild longing to live, to do what she pleased, to be free to enjoy this excitement before her wings should be clipped, and her outlook all gray and humdrum.

"I do not know if they will rest—I cannot say—I—" she blurted out tremblingly.

The stranger had put down the Times, and was gazing into her face with a look almost of tenderness.

"There is no need to answer now, " he said softly. "If fate means us to be happy, she will arrange it—I think you will come. "

Miss Rawson started to her feet, and absently put her letter to her fiance—which contained merely the sentence that they had arrived in Rome—into its envelope and fastened it up.

"I must go now—good-bye, " she said.

"It is not good-bye, " the Russian answered gravely. "By six o'clock, we shall be driving in the Borghese Gardens and hearing the nightingales sing. "

As Stella walked to the lift with a tumultuously beating heart, she asked herself what all this could possibly mean, and why she was not angry—and why this stranger—whose appearance outraged all her ideas as to what an English gentleman should look like— had yet the power to fascinate her completely. Of course, she would not go for a drive with him—and yet, what would be the harm? After September she would never have a chance like this again. There would be only Eustace Medlicott and parish duties— yes—if fate made it possible, she would go!

And she went on to her room with exhilarating sense of adventure coursing through her veins.

"I have found out the name of the peculiar-looking foreigner who sat near us last night, " Canon Ebley said, as they drove to the Lateran in a little Roman Victoria, "it is Count Roumovski; I asked the hall porter—reprehensible curiosity I fear you will think, my dear Caroline, but there is something unaccountably interesting about him, as you must admit, although you disapprove of his appearance. "

"I think it is quite dreadful, " Mrs. Ebley sniffed, "and I hear from Martha that he has no less than two valets, and a suite of princely rooms and motor cars, and the whole passage on the second floor is filled with his trunks. "

Martha had been Mrs. Ebley's maid for twenty-five years, and as Stella well knew was fairly accurate in her recounting of the information she picked up. This luridly extravagant picture, however, did not appal her. And she found herself constantly dwelling upon it and the stranger all the time she followed her relations about in the gorgeous church.

Fate did not seem to be going to smile upon the drive project, however—for Mrs. Ebley, far from appearing tired, actually proposed tea in the hall when they got in—and there sat for at least half an hour, while Stella saw Count Roumovski come in and sit down and leisurely begin a cigarette, as he glanced at an Italian paper. He was so intensely still, always peace seemed to breathe from his atmosphere, but the very sight of him appeared to exasperate the Aunt Caroline more and more.

"I wonder that man is not ashamed to be seen in a respectable place, " she snapped, "with his long hair and his bracelet—such effeminacy is perfectly disgusting, Erasmus. "

"I really cannot help it, my dear, " Canon Ebley replied, irritably, "and I rather like his face. "

"Erasmus! " was all Mrs. Ebley could say, and prepared to return to her room. Dinner would be at a quarter to eight, she told Stella at her door, and recommended an hour's quiet reading up of the guide-book while resting to her niece.

It was quarter after six before Miss Rawson descended the stairs to the hall again. She had deliberately made up her mind—she would go and drive with the count. She would live and amuse herself, if it was only for this once in her life, come what might of it! And since he would be presented with all respectable ceremony at the English Embassy the following night, it could not matter a bit—and if it did—! Well, she did not care!

He was sitting there as immovable as before, and she thrilled as she crossed the hall. She was so excited and frightened that she could almost have turned back when she reached the street, but there, standing by the trees, was a large blue motor car, and as she advanced the chauffeur stepped forward and opened the door, and she got in—and before she had time to realize what she had done, Count Roumovski had joined her and sat down by her side.

"You have no wrap, " he said. "I thought you would not have, so I had prepared this, " and he indicated a man's gray Russian, unremarkable-looking cloak, which, however, proved to be lined with fine sable, "and here, also, is a veil. If you will please me by putting them on, we can then have the auto open and no one will recognize you—even should we meet your uncle and aunt; that is fun, is it not? "

Stella had thrown every consideration to the winds, except the determination to enjoy herself. Years of rebellion at the boredom of her existence seemed to be urging her on. So she meekly slipped into the cloak, and wrapped the veil right over her hat, and they started.

Her heart was thumping so with excitement she could not have spoken for a moment.

But as they went rapidly on through the crowded streets, her companion's respectful silence reassured her. There seemed to be some rapport between them, she was conscious of a feeling that he understood her thoughts, and was not misjudging her.

"You are like a little frightened bird, " he said presently. "And there is nothing to cause you the least fear. We shall soon come to the lovely gardens, and watch the lowering sun make its beautiful effects in the trees, and we shall hear the nightingales throbbing out love songs—the world is full of rest and peace— when we have had enough passion and strife and want its change— but you do not know anything of it, and this simple drive is causing you tumults and emotions—is it not so? "

"Yes, " said Stella, with a feeling that she had burnt all her ships.

"It is because you have never been allowed to be YOU, I suppose, " he went on softly. "So doing a natural and simple thing seems frightful—because it would seem so to the rigid aunt. Now, I have been ME ever since I was born—I have done just what seemed best to me. Do you suppose I am not aware that the way my hair is cut is a shock to most civilized persons; and that you English would strongly disapprove of my watch and my many other things. But I like them myself—it is no trouble for one of my valets to draw a straight line with a pair of scissors—and if I must look at the time, I prefer to look at something beautiful. I am entirely uninfluenced by the thoughts or opinions of any people—they do not exist for me except in so far as they interest me and are instructive or amusing. I never permit myself to be bored for an instant. "

"How good that must be, " Stella ventured to say—her courage was returning.

"Civilized human beings turn existence into a prison, " he went on, meditatively, "and loaded themselves with shackles, because some convention prevents their doing what would give them innocent pleasure. If I had been under the dominion of these things we should not now be enjoying this delightful drive—at least, it is delightful to me—to be thus near you and alone out of doors. "

15

Stella did not speak, she was altogether too full of emotion to trust herself to words just yet. They had turned into the Corso by now, and, as ever, it appeared as though it were a holiday, so thronged with pedestrians was the whole thoroughfare. Count Roumovski seemed quite unconcerned, but Miss Rawson shrank back into her corner, a new fear in her heart.

"Do not be so nervous, " her companion said gently. "I always calculate the chances before I suggest another person's risking anything for me. They are a million to one that anyone could recognize you in that veil and that cloak; believe me, although I am not of your country, I am at least a gentleman, and would not have persuaded you to come if there had been any danger of complications for you. "

Stella clasped her hands convulsively—and he drew a little nearer her.

"Do put all agitating ideas out of your mind, " he said, his blue eyes, with their benign expression, seeking hers and compelling them at last to look at him. "Do you understand that it is foolish to spoil what we have by useless tremors. You are here with me— for the next hour—shall we not try to be happy? "

"Yes, " murmured Miss Rawson, and allowed herself to be magnetized into calmness.

"When we have passed the Piazza del Popolo and the entrance to the Pincio, I will have the car opened; then we can see all the charming young green, and I will tell you of what these gardens were long ago, and you shall see them with new eyes. "

Stella, by some sort of magic, seemed to have recovered her self-possession as his eyes looked into hers, and she chatted to him naturally, and the next half hour passed like some fairy tale. His deep, quiet voice took her into realms of fancy that her imagination had never even dreamed about. His cultivation was immense, and the Rome of the Caesars appeared to be as familiar to him as that of 1911.

The great beauty of the Borghese Gardens was at its height at the end of the day, the nightingales throbbed from the bushes, and the air was full of the fresh, exquisite scents of the late spring, as the day grew toward evening and all nature seemed full of beauty and peace. It can easily be imagined what this drive meant, then, to a fine, sensitive young woman, whose every instinct of youth and freedom and life had been crushed into undeveloped nothingness by years of gray convention in an old-fashioned English cathedral town.

Stella Rawson forgot that she and this Russian were strangers, and she talked to him unrestrainedly, showing glimpses of her inner self that she had not known she possessed. It was certainly heaven, she thought, this drive, and worth all the Aunt Caroline's frowns.

Count Roumovski never said a word of love to her: he treated her with perfect courtesy and infinite respect, but when at last they were turning back again, he permitted himself once more to gaze deeply into her eyes, and Stella knew for the first time in her existence that some silences are more dangerous than words.

"You do not care at all now for the good clergy-man you are affianced to, " he said. "No—do not be angry-I am not asking a question, I am stating a fact—when lives have been hedged and controlled and retenu like yours has been, even the feelings lose character, and you cannot be sure of them—but the day is approaching when you will see clearly and—feel much. "

"I am sure it is getting very late, " said Stella Rawson, and with difficulty she turned her eyes away and looked over the green world.

Count Roumovski laughed softly, as if to himself. And they were silent until they came to the entrance gates again, when the chauffeur stopped and shut the car.

"We have at least snatched some moments of pleasure, have we not? " the owner whispered, "and we have hurt no one. Will you trust me again when I propose something which sounds to you wild? "

"Perhaps I will, " Stella murmured rather low.

"When I was hunting lions in Africa I learned to keep my intelligence awake, " he said calmly, "it is an advantage to me now in civilization—nothing is impossible if one only keeps cool. If one becomes agitated one instantly connects oneself with all other currents of agitation, and one can no longer act with prudence or sense. "

"I think I have always been very foolish, " admitted Stella, looking down. "I seem to see everything differently now. "

"What we are all striving after is happiness, " Count Roumovski said. "Only we will not admit it, and nearly always spoil our own chances by drifting, and allowing outside things to influence us. If you could see the vast plains of snow in my country and the deep forests—with never a human being for miles and miles, you would understand how nature grows to talk to one—and how small the littlenesses of the world appear. " Then they were silent again, and it was not until they were rushing up the Via Nazionale and in a moment or two would have reached their destination, that Count Roumovski said:

"Stella—that means star—it is a beautiful name—I can believe you could be a star to shine upon any man's dark night—because you have a pure spirit, although it has been muffled by circumstances for all these years. "

Then the automobile drew up by the trees, at perhaps two hundred yards from the hotel, near the baths of Diocletian.

"If you will get out here, it will be best, " Count Roumovski told her respectfully, "and walk along on the inner side. I will then drive to the door of the hotel, as usual. "

"Thank you, and good-bye, " said Stella, and began untying the veil—he helped her at once, and in doing so his hand touched her soft pink cheek. She thrilled with a new kind of mad enjoyment, the like of which she had never felt, and then controlled herself and stamped it out.

"It has been a very great pleasure to me, " he said, and nothing more; no "good-bye" or "au revoir" or anything, and he drew into the far corner as she got out of the car, letting the chauffeur help her. Nor did he look her way as he drove on. And Stella walked leisurely back to the hotel, wondering in her heart at the meaning of things.

No one noticed her entrance, and she was able to begin to dress for dinner without even Martha being aware that she had been absent. But as she descended in the lift with her uncle and aunt it seemed as if the whole world and life itself were changed since the same time the night before.

And when they were entering the restaurant a telegram was put into Canon Ebley's hand—it was from the Rev. Eustace Medlicott, sent from Turin, saying he would join them in Rome the following evening.

"Eustace has been preparing this delightful surprise—I knew of it, " the Aunt Caroline said, with conscious pride, "but I would not tell you, Stella, dear, in case something might prevent it. I feared to disappoint you. "

"Thank you, aunt, " Miss Rawson said without too much enthusiasm, and took her seat where she could see the solitary occupant of a small table, surrounded by the obsequious waiters, already sipping his champagne.

He had not looked up as they passed. Nor did he appear once to glance in their direction. His whole manner was full of the same reflective calm as the night before. And, for some unaccountable reason, Stella Rawson's heart sank down lower and lower, until at the end of the repast she looked pale and tired out.

Eustace, her betrothed, would be there on the morrow, and such things as drives in motor cars with strange Russian counts were only dreams and not realities, she now felt.

CHAPTER III

Next morning it fell about that Stella Rawson was allowed to go into the Musso Nazionale in the Diocletian baths, accompanied only by Martha, her uncle and aunt having decided they would take a rest and write their English letters. The museum was so near, a mere hundred yards, there could be no impropriety in their niece's going there with Martha, even in an exhibition year in Rome.

Stella was still suffering from a nameless sense of depression. Eustace's train would get in at about five o'clock, and he would accompany them to the Embassy. A cousin of her own and Aunt Caroline's was one of the secretaries, and had already been written to about the invitation. So that even if Count Roumovski should be presented to her, and make the whole thing proper and correct, she would have no chance of any conversation. The brilliant sunlight felt incongruous and hurt her, and she was glad to enter the shady ancient baths. She had glanced furtively to right and left in the hotel as she came through the hall, but saw no one who resembled the Russian, and they had walked so quickly through the vestibule she had not remarked a tall figure coming from the staircase, nor had seen him give some rapid order to a respectful servant who was waiting about, and who instantly followed them: but if she had looked up as she paid for the two tickets at the barrier of the museum, she would have seen this same lean man turn swiftly round and retreat in the direction of the hotel.

Martha was sulky and comatose on this very warm morning; she took no interest in sculpture. "Them naked creatures, " she called any masterpiece undraped—and she resented being dragged out by Miss Stella, who always had fancies for art.

They walked round the cloisters first, a voyage of discovery to Miss Rawson, who looked a slim enough nymph herself in her lilac cambric frock and demure gray hat shading her big brown eyes.

Then suddenly, from across the garden in the center, she became aware that an archaic Apollo clad in modern dress had entered upon the scene, and the blood rushed to her cheeks, and her heart beat.

Martha puffed with the heat and exercise, and glanced with longing eyes at a comfortable stone bench in the shade.

"Would you like to rest here, Martha, you old dear? " Miss Rawson said. "There is not a creature about, and I will walk round and join you from the other side. "

The Aunt Caroline's elderly maid easily agreed to this. It was true there did not seem to be anyone adventurous-looking, and Miss Stella would be more or less under her eye—and she was thoroughly tired with traveling and what not. So Stella found herself happily unchaperoned, except by Baedecker, as she strolled on.

The Russian had disappeared from view, the bushes and vases in the center of the garden plot gave only occasional chances to see people at a distance.

But when Stella had entered the Ludovici collection she perceived him to the right, gazing at the statue of the beautiful Mars.

He turned instantly, as though some one told him she was near— and his calm eyes took in the fact that she was alone. The small room was empty but for the two, and he addressed her as he removed his hat.

"Good morning, mademoiselle, " he said gravely. "Mars is a strong attraction. I knew I should presently find you here—so when I caught sight of your spiritual outline across the garden, I came and— waited. "

"He is most splendid-looking, is he not, " Stella returned, trying to suppress the sudden tingle of pleasure that was thrilling her, "and look how much character there is in his hands. "

"Shall we go and study the others, or shall we find a bench in the garden and sit down and talk? " Count Roumovski asked serenely, and then smiled to himself as he noticed his companion's apprehensive glance in the direction where, far away, Martha dozed in peace.

"It would be nice out of doors—but—" and Stella faltered.

"Do not let us be deprived of pleasure by any buts—there is one out there who will warn us when your maid wakes. See—" and he advanced toward the entrance door, "there is a bench by that rose tree where we can be comparatively alone. "

Stella struggled no more with herself. After all, it was her last chance—Eustace Medlicott's train got in at five o'clock!

She had a sense of security, too, the complete serenity of her companion inspired confidence. She almost felt she would not care if Aunt Caroline herself slept instead of the elderly maid.

There was some slight change in Count Roumovski's manner to-day— he kept his eyes fixed upon her face, and the things he said were less abstract and more personal. After an entrancing half hour she felt she had seen vivid pictures of his land and his home. But he was a great traveler it appeared, and had not been there often in later years.

"It is so agreeable to let the body move from place to place, and remain in a peaceful aloofness of the spirit all the time, " he said at last. "To watch all the rushing currents which dominate human beings when they do not know how to manipulate them. If they did, the millennium would come, —but, meanwhile, it is reserved for the few who have learned them to enjoy this present plane we are on. "

"You mean you can control events and shape your life as you please, then? " Stella asked surprised, while she raised her sweet shy eyes to his inquiringly. "I wish I knew how! "

"Shall I try to teach you, mademoiselle? " he said.

"Yes, indeed. "

"Then you must not look down all the time, even though the contemplation of your long eyelashes gives me a pleasure—I would prefer the eyes themselves—the eyes are the indication of what is passing in the soul, and I would study this moving panorama. "

Stella's color deepened, but she met his blue orbs without flinching—so he went on:

"I had the fortune to be born a Russian, which has given me time to study these things. My country does not require my work beyond my being a faithful servant of my Emperor. Since I am not a soldier, I can do as I choose. But you in England are now in a seething caldron, and it would be difficult, no doubt, for you to spend the hours required—although the national temperament would lend itself to all things calm if it were directed. "

"But for myself, " Stella demanded, "I am not a man, and need not interest myself in the nation's affairs—how can I grow to guide my own—as you seem to do? "

"Never permit yourself to be ruffled by anything to commence with, " Count Roumovski began gravely, while the pupils of his eyes appeared to grow larger. "Whatever mood you are in, you connect yourself with the cosmic current of that mood—you become in touch, so to speak, with all the other people who are under its dominion, and so it gains strength because unity is strength. If you can understand that as a basic principle, you can see that it is only a question of controlling yourself and directing your moods with those currents whose augmentation can bring you good. You must never be negative and drift. You can be drawn in any adverse way if you do. "

"I think I understand, " said Stella, greatly interested.

"Then you must use your critical faculties and make selections of what is best—and you must encourage common sense and distrust altruism. Sanity is the thing to aim at. "

"Yes. "

"The view of the world has become so distorted upon almost every point which started in good, that nothing but a cultivation of our individual critical faculties can enable us to see the truth—and nine-tenths of civilized humanity have no real opinion of their own at all—they simply echo those of others. "

"I feel that is true, " said Stella, thinking of her own case.

"It is not because a thing is bad or good that it succeeds—merely how much strength we put into the desire for it, " he went on.

"But surely we must believe that good will win over evil, " and the brown eyes looked almost troubled, and his softened as he looked at her.

"The very fact of believing that would make it come to pass by all these psychic laws. Whatever we really believe we draw, " he said almost tenderly.

"Then, if I were to believe all the difficulties and uncertainties would be made straight and just go on calmly, I should be happy, should I? " she asked, and there was an unconscious pathos in her voice which touched him deeply.

"Certainly, " he answered. "You have not had a fair chance—probably you have never been allowed to do a single thing of your own accord—have you? "

"N—no, " said Stella.

"In the beginning, were you engaged to this good clergyman of your own wish? " and his eyes searched her face.

She stiffened immediately, the training of years took offense, and she answered rather stiffly:

"I do not think you have the right to ask me such a question, Count Roumovski. "

He was entirely unabashed—he stroked his pointed silky beard for a moment, then he said calmly:

"Yes—I have, you agreed that I should teach you how to shape your life as you pleased, you must remember. It is rather essential that I should know the truth of this matter before I can go further—you must see that. "

"We can avoid the subject. "

"It would be Hamlet without Hamlet, then, " he smiled. "One could draw up no scheme of rules and exercises, unless one has some idea of how far the individual was responsible for the present state of things. If it was your wish in the beginning, or if you were coerced makes all the difference. "

Stella was silent—only she nervously plucked an offending rose which grew upon a bush beside them: she pulled its petals off and kept her eyes lowered, and Sasha Roumovski smiled a wise smile.

"You have unconsciously answered me, " he said, "and your agitation proves that not only are you aware that you did not become engaged of your own wish, but that you are afraid to face the fact and admit that its aspect appals you. You must remember, in your country, where, I understand, divorce is not tres bien vu, especially among the clergy, the affair is for life, and the joy or the gall of it could be infinite. "

She raised two beseeching eyes to his face at last.

"Oh, do not let us talk about it, " she pleaded. "It is so warm and pleasant here—I want to be happy. "

He looked at her for a while with penetrating eyes, then he said gently:

"It is a man's province to take care of a woman, " and his attractive voice filled with a new cadence. "I see you are in need of direction. Leave all to me—and forget there is any one else in the world for the moment but our two selves. Did you know that I thought you looked particularly sweet last night, but rather pale? "

"You never looked at me at all, " said Stella before she was aware of it, and then blushed crimson at the inference of her speech. He would be able to understand perfectly that she must have been observing him all the time to be conscious of this.

A gleam of gladness came into his eyes.

"I would like to watch you always openly, if I might, " he whispered. "Your little face is like a flower in its delicate tints, and your eyes are true and tender and asking so many questions of life, —and sometimes they are veiled and misty, and then they look wise and courageous. I am beginning to know all their changes. "

"Then, in that case, monotony will set in, " Stella was almost arch— the day was so glorious!

"I am not afraid of that, " he said. "I always know what I want and what is worth while. I do not value my three matchless pearls the less because I know their every iridescence—on the contrary, I grow more fond of them and wear them every night in preference to any others. "

They were silent for a moment after this. He was examining her minutely with his wise, calm eyes. He was noting the sensitive curve of the pretty full lips, the tender droop of the set of her head, the gracious charm of her little regular features, and the intelligence of her broad brow. With all her simplicity, she looked no fool or weakling. And to think that the narrow code of those who surrounded her should force this sweet young creature into the gray walls of a prison house, when she became the English clergyman's wife; it was too revolting to him. Count Roumovski suddenly made up his mind, trained to instantaneous decision by his bent of studies, and sure and decided in its action. And if Stella had looked up then she would have seen a keen gleam in the peaceful blue of his eyes. He drew her on to talk of her home and her tastes—she loved many things he did, he found—and she was so eager to hear and to learn their meaning. He grew to feel a sort of pride and the pleasure of a teacher when directing an extremely intelligent child. There were no barriers of stupidity into whatever regions the subjects might wander. They spent an hour of pure joy investigating each other's thoughts. And both knew they were growing more than friends.

Then Stella rose suddenly to her feet. A clock struck twelve.

"You said one must not be negative and drift, " she announced demurely, "so I am being decided and must now go to Martha again. "

"Ivan has not warned us that she is thinking of stirring, " Count Roumovski said. "I told him to, and he will let us know in plenty of time; you surely do not breakfast until half-past twelve, do you? "

"Ivan? —who is Ivan? " Stella asked.

"He is a servant of mine who does what he is bid, " her companion answered. "To have peace to enjoy oneself one must calculate and arrange for events. Had we only trusted to the probability of your maid's sleeping, I should have had to be on the lookout, and my uneasiness would have communicated itself to you, and we should have had no happy hour—but I made a certainty of safety—and unconsciously you trusted me to know, and so we have been content. "

Stella was thrilled. So he had taken all this trouble. He must be a good deal interested in her, then; and feeling sure of this, womanlike, she immediately took advantage of it to insist upon leaving him.

"Very well, " he said, when he could not dissuade her. "To-night the wheel of fortune will revolve for us all, and it remains to be seen who will draw a prize and who a blank. "

Then he walked by her side to where they saw the quiet servant standing, a motionless sentinel, and here Count Roumovski bowed and turned on his heel, while Stella advanced to the bench on which the comfortable Martha slept.

This latter was full of defence when she awoke. She had not closed an eye, but thought Miss Stella was enjoying "them statues" better without her, which was indeed true, if she had guessed!

Miss Rawson ate very little luncheon—the Russian did not appear—and immediately after it she was taken as a treat to see the Borghese Gardens by her uncle and aunt! It behooved her not to be tired by more sightseeing, since her betrothed would arrive when they returned for tea, and would expect her to be bright and on the alert to please him, Aunt Caroline felt. As for Stella, as that moment approached it seemed to her that the end of all joy had come.

CHAPTER IV

The Rev. Eustace Medlicott, when the stains of travel had been removed from his thin person, came down to tea in the hall of the Grand Hotel with a distinct misgiving in his heart. He did not approve of it as a place of residence for his betrothed. Another and equally well-drained hostelry might have been found for the party he thought, where such evidences of worldly occupations and amusements would not so forcibly strike the eye. Music with one's meals savored of paganism. He was still very emaciated with his Lenten fast. It took him until July, generally, to pick up again; and he was tired with his journey. Stella was not there to greet him, only the Aunt Caroline, and he felt a sense of injury creeping over him. She might have been in time. Nancy Ruggles, the Bishop's second daughter, had given him tea and ministered to his wants in a spirit of solicitous devotion every day since the Ebleys had left Exminster, but Nancy's hair was not full of sunlight, nor did her complexion suggest cream and roses. Things which, to be sure, the Rev. Eustace Medlicott felt he ought not to dwell upon; they were fleshly lusts and should be discouraged.

He had been convinced that celibacy was the only road to salvation for a priest, until Stella Rawson's fair young charms had unconsciously undermined this conviction. But even if he had been able to arrange his conscience to his liking upon the vital point, he felt he must fight bravely against allowing himself or his betrothed to get any pleasure out of the affair. It was better to marry than to burn, he had St. Paul's authority for this—but when he felt emotion toward Stella because of her loveliness, he was afterward very uncomfortable in his thoughts, and it took him at least an hour to throw dust in his own eyes in regard to the nature of his desire for her, which he determined to think was only of the spirit. Love, for him, was no god to be exalted, but a too strong beast to be resisted, and every one of his rites were to be succumbed to shamefacedly and under protest. Thus did he criticize the scheme of his Creator like many another before him.

He sat now in the hall of the Grand Hotel at Rome feeling ill at ease and expressed some mild disapproval of the surroundings to Mrs. Ebley, who fired up at once. She was secretly enjoying herself extremely, and allowed the drains to assume gigantic proportions in her reasons for their choice of abode. So there was nothing more to be said, and Stella, looking rather pale, presently came down the steps from the corridor where their lift was situated, and joined the group in the far corner of the large hall.

She was so slender and fresh and graceful, and, even in the week's sight-seeing in Paris, she seemed to have picked up a new air, though she wore the same gray Sunday dress her fiance was accustomed to see at home—it appeared to be put on differently, and she had altered the doing of her hair. There was no doubt about it, his future wife was a most delectable-looking creature, but these tendencies toward adornment of the person which he observed must be checked at once.

They shook hands with decorous cordiality, and Stella sat down demurely in the vacant chair. She felt as cold as ice toward him, and looked it more or less. It made Mr. Medlicott nervous, although she answered gently enough when he addressed her. Inwardly she was trying to overcome the growing revulsion she was experiencing. Tricks of speech, movements of hands—even the way Eustace's hair grew—were all irritating her. She only longed to contradict every word the poor man said, and she felt wretched and unjust and at war with herself and fate. At last things almost came to a point when he moved his chair so that he should be close to her and a little apart from the others, and whispered with an air of absolute proprietorship:

"My little Stella has changed her sweetly modest way of hairdressing. I hardly think the new style is suitable to my retiring dove. "

"Why, it is only parted in the middle and brushed back into a simple knot, " Miss Rawson retorted, with sparkling eyes. "How can you be so ridiculous, Eustace—it is merely because it is becoming and more in the fashion that you object, there is nothing the least remarkable in the style itself. "

Mr. Medlicott's thin lips grew into a straight line.

"It is that very point—the suggestion of fashion that I object to—the wife of a clergyman cannot be too careful not to make herself attractive or remarkable in any way, " he said sententiously, his obstinate chin a little forward.

"But I am not a clergyman's wife yet, " said Stella with some feeling, "and can surely enjoy a few things of my age until I am— and doing my hair how I please is one of them. "

Mr. Medlicott shrugged his shoulders, he refused to continue this unseemly altercation with his betrothed. He would force her to see reason when once she should be his wife, until then he might have to waive his authority, but should show her by his manner that she had offended him, and judging from the attitudes of the adoring spinsters he had left at Exminster that should be punishment enough.

He turned to the Aunt Caroline now and addressed her exclusively and Stella rebelliously moved her seat back a few inches and looked across the room; and at that moment the tall, odd-looking Russian came in, and retired to a seat far on the other side, exactly opposite them. Here he ordered a hock and seltzer with perfect unconcern, and smoked his cigarette. Miss Rawson could hardly bear it.

"There is that extraordinary man again, Stella, " Mrs. Ebley turned to her and said. "I thought he had gone as he was not at luncheon to-day. I am sure your fiance will agree with me that such an appearance is sacrilegious—he must know he looks like a saint— and I am quite sure, from what I have heard from Martha, he is not one at all. He lives in the greatest luxury, Eustace, " she continued, turning to the Rev. Mr. Medlicott. "and probably does no good to anyone in the world. "

"How can you suppose that, Aunt Caroline, " Stella answered with some spirit, "it is surely very uncharitable to judge of people by their appearances and—and what Martha repeats to you. "

Mrs. Ebley gasped—never in her whole life had her niece spoken to her in this tone. She to be rebuked! It was unspeakable. She could only glare behind her glasses. What had come to the girl in the last two days—if this manner was the result of travel, far better to have stayed at home!

Here Canon Ebley joined in, hoping to bring peace:

"You have told Eustace what is in store for him to-night, have you not, Caroline, my dear? " he asked. "We have to put on our best and take our ladies to the Embassy to a rout, Eustace, " he went on, genially. "There are a Russian Grand Duke and Duchess passing through, it appears, who are going to be entertained. "

"There will be no dancing, I suppose, " said Mr. Medlicott primly, "because, if so, I am sorry, but I cannot accompany you—it is not that I disapprove of dancing for others, " he hastened to add, "but I do not care to watch it myself. And I do not think it wise for Stella to grow to care for it, either. "

"It is merely a reception, " Mrs. Ebley said, "and it will be a very interesting sight. "

Stella sat silent; she was overcome with the whole situation; and her fiance grew more distasteful to her every moment—how had she ever been persuaded to be engaged to such a person! —while the attraction of the strange-looking Russian seemed to increase. In spite of the grotesque hair and unusual beard, there was an air of great distinction about him. His complete unconsciousness and calm were so remarkable. You might take him for an eccentric person, but certainly a gentleman, and with an extraordinary magnetism, she felt. When once you had talked to him, he seemed to cast a spell over you. But, beyond this, she only knew that she was growing more unhappy every moment, and that by her side one man represented everything that was tied and bound in sentiment and feeling and existence, and that across the hall another opened the windows of her reason and imagination, and exhorted her to be free, and herself.

Presently she could bear it no more. She got up rather suddenly, and, saying she was very tired and had letters to write, she left them and went toward the lift.

"Stella is not at all like herself, " Mr. Medlicott said, when she had disappeared from view. "I trust she is not sickening with Roman fever. "

Meanwhile, Miss Rawson had reached her room and pulled her writing case in front of her. There were one or two girl friends who ought to be written to, but the sheets remained blank—and in about ten minutes there was a gentle knock at the door, and, on opening it, she saw Count Roumovski's discreet-looking servant, who handed her a note respectfully, and then went on his way without a word.

How agreeable it must be to have well-trained servants to do one's bidding like that! she thought, and then went back eagerly to her window to read the missive. It had no beginning or date, and was just a few lines.

I have observed the whole situation, and judged of the character of your fiance. I know how you feel. Do not be depressed—remain calm and trust me, circumstances can always be directed in the hands of a strong man. I will have the honor to be presented to you and to your family soon after you arrive at the Embassy to- night. All is well.

There was no signature, and the writing was rather large and unlike any she had seen before.

Suddenly her feeling of unrest left her, and a lightness of heart took its place. She was living, at all events, and the horizon was not all gray. It seemed almost delightful to be putting on a real evening dress presently, even though it was a rather homely white thing with a pink sash, and to be going down to the restaurant in it with Aunt Caroline in front in her best black velvet and point lace.

That lady's desire to be in time at the party alone determined her to this breach of the rules—and there were Eustace and Uncle Erasmus in their stiff clerical evening coats awaiting them in the corridor— while, as luck would have it, the lift stopped at the second floor to admit the Russian. He got in with his usual air of being unaware that he was not alone—though Stella could feel that he was touching her hand—perhaps unconsciously. He seemed to radiate some kind of joy for her always, and the pink grew to that of a June rose in her cheeks, and her brown eyes shone like two stars.

"That was the man you spoke of in the hall, Mrs. Ebley, was it not? " Eustace Medlicott's intoning voice said, as they went along to the restaurant. "He certainly is a most remarkable person to look at close—but I do not dislike his face, it has noble lines. "

"Really, how condescending of you! " Stella almost said aloud. But the Aunt Caroline answered serenely:

"Perhaps I am prejudiced, Eustace, but want of convention always shocks me to such a degree that I cannot appreciate anything else. "

Stella almost enjoyed her dinner, she was so excited with the prospect of some unknown coming events, and she had the satisfaction of observing that once Count Roumovski actually turned his head in their direction and met her eyes. His were full of a whimsical smile for the instant he looked, and then he relapsed into his habitual indifference.

The crowd had begun to thicken when they got to the Embassy, and they waited among them for the Royalties' arrival; Stella looking at everything with fresh, interested eyes. When this ceremony was over people began to disperse about the large rooms, and Miss Rawson was conscious that her strange secret acquaintance was in conversation with the Grand Duke and Duchess; she had not seen him come in. The Aunt Caroline noticed this, too, and drew her attention to the fact.

"Look, Stella, that dreadful man is talking to Royalty! " she said. "I suppose he must be a gentleman, after all—one never can tell with foreigners, as their titles mean nothing, and half of them are assumed. Your Uncle Carford had a valet once who afterward was arrested for posing as a Polish count. "

"I should think anyone could see this man was a gentleman, Aunt Caroline, " Stella answered, "even without his talking to Royalties. "

They were soon joined by the secretary cousin, who was charmed to welcome so pretty a relation to Rome, and was profuse in his apologies for not having been able to do more than leave cards upon them as yet.

"We should so like to know the names of the celebrities, " Mrs. Ebley said, "especially can you tell us about the very curious- looking person now conversing with her Imperial Highness; he is at our hotel. "

"That—Oh! that is by far the most interesting man here—it is the famous Count Roumovski. He is a most celebrated traveler; he has been all over the world and Africa and Asia in unaccessible places. He is a fabulously rich Russian—a real Muscovite from near Moscow, and he does everything and anything he pleases; he gives enormous sums for the encouragement of science. He is immensely intelligent—he lunched at the Embassy to-day. "

"Really! " said the Aunt Caroline, somewhat impressed. "His appearance is greatly against him. "

"Oh, do you think so? " said the cousin. "I think it adds to his attraction, it is such superlative audacity. No Englishman would have the nerve to cut his hair like that. "

"I should hope not, " said Mrs. Ebley severely, and dropped the subject.

"To think of this charming rosebud of a girl going to marry Eustace Medlicott—insufferable, conceited prig, I remember him at Oxford, " the cousin was musing to himself. "Lord Carford is an old stick-in-the-mud, or he would have prevented that. She is his own niece, and one can see by her frock that the poor child never even goes to London. "

At this moment they saw the Russian Count putting his heels together and bowing himself out of the circle of his Royalties; and straight as a dart he came over to where their group was standing, and whispered in the cousin's—Mr. Deanwood's ear—who then asked if he might present Count Roumovski to the Aunt Caroline and the rest.

When this ceremony was over Mrs. Ebley found herself conversing with her whilom object of contempt, and coming gradually under the influence of his wonderful charm, while Stella stood there trembling with the wildest excitement she had yet known. The words of Eustace, her betrothed, talking to her, carried no meaning to her brain, her whole intelligence was strung up to catch what the others were saying.

With great dexterity the Russian presently made the conversation general, and drew her into it, and then he said with composure that the Gardens were illuminated—and, as it was such a very hot night, would mademoiselle like to take a turn that way, to have some refreshment? At the same moment, Mr. Deanwood gave Mrs. Ebley his arm, and they all moved forward—followed by Canon Ebley and the Rev. Eustace Medlicott, with no great joy upon his face.

Stella, meanwhile, felt herself being drawn rapidly ahead, and so maneuvered that in a moment or two they had completely lost sight of the rest of the relations, and were practically alone in a crowd.

"At last! " Count Roumovski whispered, "even I, who am generally calm, was beginning to feel I should rush over, throw prudence to the winds and—" then he stopped abruptly, and Stella felt her heart thump in her throat, while her little hand on his arm was pressed against his side.

They made the pretense of taking some refreshment at the buffet, and then went toward the open doors of the garden. The part all round the house was illuminated, and numbers of people strolled about, the night was deliciously warm. Count Roumovski seemed to know the paths, for he drew his companion to a seat just beyond the radius of the lights, and they sat down upon a bench under a giant tree. He had not spoken a word, but now he leaned back and deliberately looked into her eyes, while his voice, with vibrations of feeling in it which thrilled Stella, whispered in her ear:

"It cannot go on, of course—you agree with me about that, do you not? "

"What cannot go on? " she asked, to gain time to recover her composure.

"This situation, " he answered. "I am sure now that I love you—and I want to teach you a number of things, first in importance being that you shall love me. "

"Oh, you must not say this, " Stella protested feebly.

"Yes, I must, and you will listen to me, little star. "

He drew nearer to her, and the amazing power of propinquity began to assert itself. She felt as if the force to resist him were leaving her, she was trembling all over with delicious thrills.

"I made up my mind almost immediately I saw you, sweet child, " he went on, "that you were what I have been waiting for all my life. You are good and true—and balanced—or you will be that when I have made your love education. Stella, look at me with those soft eyes, and tell me that I mean something to you already, and that the worthy Mr. Medlicott does not exist any more. "

"I—I—but I have only known you for two days, " Stella answered confusedly: she was so full of emotion that she dared not trust herself further.

"Does time count, then, so much with conventional people? " he demanded. "For me it has no significance in relation to feeling. If you would only look at me instead of down at those small hands, then you would not be able to tell me these foolish things! "

This was so true that Stella could not deny it, her breath came rather fast; it was the supreme moment her life had yet known.

"You are frightened because the training of your education still holds you and not nature. Your acquired opinion tells you you are engaged to another man, and ought not to listen to me. "

"Of course I ought not to, " she murmured.

"Of course you ought—how else can you come to any conclusion if you do not hear my arguments—sweet, foolish one! "

She did look at him now with two startled eyes.

"Listen attentively, darling pupil, and sweet love, " he said. He was leaning with one arm on the back of the bench supporting his head on his hand, turned quite toward her, who sat with clasped nervous fingers clutching her fan. His other hand lay idly on his knee, his whole attitude was very still. The soft lights were just enough for him to see distinctly her small face and shining hair; his own face was in shadow, but she could feel the magnetism of his eyes penetrating through her very being.

"You were coerced by those in charge of you, " he went on in a level voice of argument, which yet broke into notes of tenderness, "you were influenced into becoming engaged to this man who is ridiculously unsuited to you. You, so full of life and boundless joy! You, who will learn all of love's meaning presently, and what it makes of existence, and what God meant by giving it to us mortals. You are intended by nature to be a complete woman if you did but know it—but such a life, tied to that half fish man, would atrophy all that is finest in your character. You would grow really into what they are trying to make you appear—after years of hopelessness and suffering. Do you not feel all this, little star, tell me? "

"Yes, " Stella answered, "it is true—I have seemed to feel the cords and the shackles pulling at me often, but never that they were unbearable until I—spoke with you—and you put new thoughts into my head. "

"I did well, then. And because of a silly convention you would ruin all your life by going on with these ways—it is unthinkable! " and his deep voice vibrated with feeling. "It is a mistake, that is all, and can be rectified, —if you were already married to this man I would not plead so, because then you would have crossed the Rubicon, and assumed responsibilities which you would have to accept or suffer the consequences. But this preliminary bond can be broken without hurt to either side. A man of the good clergyman's type will not suffer in his emotions at the loss of you—he suffices unto himself for those; his vanity will be wounded—that is all. And surely it is better that should gall for a little than that you should spoil your life. Sweet flower, realize yourself these things—that sunny hair and that beautiful skin and those velvet eyes were made for the joy and glory of a man—not for temptations to a strict priest, who would resent their power as a sin every time he felt himself influenced by their charm. Gods above! he would not know what to do with you, heart of me! "

Stella was thrilling with exquisite emotion, but the influence of her strict and narrow bringing up could not be quite overcome in these few moments. She longed to be convinced, and yet some altruistic sentiment made her feel still some qualms and misgivings. If she should be causing Eustace great pain by breaking her engagement; if it were very wrong to go against her uncle and aunt—especially her Aunt Caroline, her own mother's sister. She clasped her little hands nervously, and looked up in this strong man's face with pathetic, pleading intensity.

"Oh, please tell me, what ought I to do, then—what is right? " she implored. "And because I want so much to believe you, I fear it must be wrong to do so. "

He leaned nearer to her and spoke earnestly. His stillness was almost ominous, it gave the impression of such immense self- control, and his voice was as those bass notes of the priests of St. Isaac's in his own northern land.

"Dear, honest little girl, " he said tenderly, "I worship your goodness. And I know you will presently see the truth. Love is of God and is imperious, and because she loves him is the only reason why a woman should give her life to a man. Quite apart from the law, which proclaims that each individual must be the arbiter of his own fate, and not succumb to the wishes of others, it would be an ethical sin for you to marry the worthy Mr. Medlicott—not loving him. Surely, you can see this. "

"Yes—yes, it would be dreadful, " she murmured, "but Aunt Caroline—she caused me to accept him—I mean, she wanted me to so much. I never really felt anything for him myself, and lately— ever since the beginning, in fact, I have been getting more and more indifferent to him. "

"Then, surely, it is plain that you must be free of him, darling. Throw all the responsibility upon me, if you will. I promise to take every care of you. And I want you only to promise you will follow each step that I explain to you—" then he broke off, and the seriousness of his tone changed to one of caressing tenderness. "But first I must know for certain, little star, shall I be able to teach you to love me— as I shall love you? "

"Yes, " was all Stella could utter, and then, gaining more voice, she went on, "I did not know—I could not guess what that would mean—to love—but—"

He answered her with fond triumph:

"Now you are beginning to understand, darling child—that is enough for me to know for the present. In your country, a man asks a woman to marry him: he says, 'Will you marry me? '—is it not so? of course, I need not say that to you, because you know that is what I mean. When these wearisome thongs are off your wrists you will belong to me, and come with me into my country and be part of my life. "

"Ah! " whispered Stella, the picture seemed one of heaven, that was all.

"You must have freedom to assert your individuality, Stella, " he continued. "I can but show you the way and give you a new point of view, but I will never try to rule you and drag you to mine. I will never put any chains upon you but those of love. Do they sound as if they would be too heavy, dearest? "

"I think not, " she said very low. "I feel as though I were looking into a beautiful garden from the top of an ugly, barren, cold mountain. I shall like to come down and go in among the unknown flowers. "

"It will be so glorious for us, " he said exultantly, "because we have still all the interesting things to find out about each other, —" And then, her sweet face so very near him, the temptation to caress her became too intense; he quivered and changed his position, clasping his hands.

"Darling, " he said hoarsely, "we must soon go back to the company, because, although I count always upon my will to make my actions obey it, still I can hardly prevent myself from seizing you in my arms and kissing your tender lips—and that I must not do—as yet. "

Stella drew herself together, the temptation was convulsing her also, though she did not guess it. She looked up into his blue eyes there in the shadow, and saw the deep reverence in them, and she understood and loved him with her soul.

He did not so much as touch her dress; indeed, now that he had won his fight, he moved a little further from her—and resumed his calm voice:

"The first thing we shall do is to stroll back through the people and find the aunt—I will then leave you with her, and soon it will be time to go home. Do not make much conversation with any of them to-night—leave everything to me. I will see the Rev. Mr. Medlicott when we return to the hotel. Whatever they say to you to-morrow, remain firm in your simple determination to break your engagement. Argue with them not at all. I will see your uncle in the morning and demand your hand; they will be shocked, horrified, scandalized—we will make no explanations. If they refuse their consent, then you must be brave, and the day after to-morrow you must come to my sister. She will have arrived by then; she was in Paris, and I telegraphed for her to join me immediately; the Princess Urazov she is called. She will receive you with affection, and you will stay with her until the formalities can be arranged, when we shall be married, and—but I cannot permit myself to think of the joy of that—for the moment. "

Stella's eyes, with trust and love, were now gazing into his, and he rose abruptly to his feet.

"You may, when you are alone, again think that it is heartless to go quite contrary to your relations like this, because they have brought you up, but remember that marriage is an act which can mean almost life or death to a woman, and that no human beings have any right to coerce you in this matter. You are of age and so am I, and we are only answerable to God and to the laws of our countries, not to individuals. "

"I will try to think of it like that, " said Stella, greatly moved, and then, with almost childish irrelevance, which touched him deeply, she asked, "What must I call you, please? "

"Oh, you sweetest star! " he exclaimed, "do not tempt me too strongly—I love you wildly and I want to fold you in my arms—and explain everything with your little head here on my breast—but I must not—must not yet. Call me Sasha—say it now that I may hear its sound in your tender voice—and we must fly, fly back to the lights—or I cannot answer for myself. "

She whispered it softly, and a shiver ran through all his tall frame— and he said, with tender masterfulness:

"Say, 'Sasha, I love, '" and this she did, also—and then he almost brusquely placed her hand upon his arm, and led her among the people, and so to her frowning relations, and then he bowed a correct good-night.

CHAPTER V

No one could have been more surprised than the Reverend Eustace Medlicott at the behavior of his betrothed. Far from showing any contrition for her unseemly absence upon the arm of a perfect stranger, and a foreigner to boot, Stella had returned to the fold of her relations' group with a demure and radiant face, and when Eustace had ventured some querulous reproaches, she had cut him short by saying she had done as she wished and did not intend to listen to any remarks about it.

"You will have to learn more humbleness of mind, my dear child, " he retorted sternly. "I cannot allow you to reply to your future husband in this independent tone. "

"I shall just answer as I please, " said Stella, and felt almost inclined to laugh, he looked so cross and amazed. Then she turned and talked to the cousin, Mr. Deanwood, and took no further notice of him.

Mr. Medlicott burned with annoyance. Stella would really have to be careful or he would not go on with the match—he had no intention of taking to wife a woman who would defy him—there was Nancy Ruggles ready to be his slave—and others besides her. And his career could be just as well assisted by the Bishop's daughter as by Canon Ebley's niece, even though her uncle was a crotchety and unknown Lord, patron of two fat livings. But Stella, with a rebellious little curl loosened on her snowy neck and a rebellious pout upon her cherry lips, was so very alluring a creature to call one's own, the desire of the flesh, which he called by any other name, fought hard with his insulted spirit, though to give in would be too ignominious; she must say she was sorry first, and then he could find it in his heart to forgive her. But the opportunity to show this magnanimity was not vouchsafed to him by fate—for other people were introduced to the party by Mr. Deanwood, and he did not exchange a word alone with his erring fiancee until she said a cold good-night in the hall of the Grand Hotel.

"Stella, remain for a moment, I wish to speak to you, " he said in the voice in which he was accustomed to read the burial service.

But she feigned not to hear and followed her Aunt Caroline's black velvet train on to the lift and at that same moment a discreet- looking foreign servant came up and handed him a note.

He read it in surprise—who could be sending him a note at a quarter past twelve at night?

Dear Sir [it ran],

I shall be greatly obliged if you can spare to me half an hour before retiring to your rest to converse upon a matter of importance. I had the honor of making your acquaintance to-night at your Embassy. If you will grant me this favor I will wait upon you immediately in the hall, or, if you prefer, my sitting-room; my servant could conduct you here, and we shall have the advantage of being entirely undisturbed. I remain, sir, Yours truly.

SASHA ROUMOVSKI.

Eustace Medlicott gasped with astonishment. This Russian gentleman was evidently in need of his ministrations and perhaps advice. He would go to his room, certainly, there were still some people in the hall having late coffee and refreshment after the theater.

He indicated by a condescending movement that he was ready to follow the waiting servant, and soon found himself being shown into Count Roumovski's sitting-room. It was luxuriously appointed and represented every appearance of manly comfort. There were quantities of books and papers about and the smell of excellent cigars, and put carelessly aside were various objets d'art which antique dealers had evidently sent for his grand seigneur's approval.

Count Roumovski was standing by the mantelpiece and looked very tall and commanding in his evening dress.

"It is most good of you to come, " he said, while he indicated a big arm-chair for his visitor to sit in—he did not offer to shake hands. "It was certainly my duty to have called upon you, my only apology for getting you to ascend here is that the subject I wish to converse with you is too serious for both of us to admit of interruptions. "

"Indeed, " said Mr. Medlicott, pompously—growing more surprised each moment. "And may I ask the nature of your trouble? "

Count Roumovski did not change his position by the mantelpiece and he kept still as a bronze statue as he spoke in a courteous tone:

"It is not a trouble at all, " he began, gravely, "on the contrary, it is a great joy and honor for me. I will state the facts immediately. I understand that for a short while you have been engaged to be married to Miss Stella Rawson, the niece of the respected English clergyman, the Reverend Ebley—"

"Pardon me, " interrupted Mr. Medlicott acidly, "but I do not see how my private affairs can interest you, sir, I cannot—"

But the host in turn interrupted him.

"If you will be so good as to listen patiently, you will find that this matter is of vital importance—may I proceed? "

Mr. Medlicott bowed; what more could he do? Count Roumovski went on:

"I understand that Miss Rawson never showed very strong affection for you or great desire for this union—so what I have to ask now is, if you, as a gentleman, will release her from her promise to you and set her free. "

"Upon my word, sir, this is too much, " Mr. Medlicott exclaimed, starting to his feet, "by what authority do you say these preposterous things? You were only introduced to Miss Rawson and myself to-night. You must be mad! "

"No, I am quite sane. And I say them upon the best authority, " Count Roumovski continued, "because I love Miss Rawson myself, and I am deeply honored by believing that in return she loves me— not you at all. Therefore, it is common sense to ask you to release her, and let her be happy with the person she prefers—is it not so? "

Eustace Medlicott had grown white with anger and astonishment as he listened, and now broke in hotly, forgetful of his intoning voice or anything but his outraged dignity.

"When have you had the opportunity to try and undermine the faith of my betrothed, may I ask? Supposing you are saying this seriously and not as some ill-timed jest. "

Count Roumovski lifted his eyebrows a little and looked almost with pity at his adversary. "We are not talking in the heroic manner, " he replied, unmoved by the other's taunt, "we are, I presume, two fairly intelligent men discussing this affair together—there has been no question of undermining. Miss Rawson and myself found we understood each other very soon after we first met. Surely, you must realize, sir, that love cannot be commanded, it will not come or go at one's bidding. These ridiculous bonds of convention, holding to a promise given when the spirit to keep it is no longer there, can ruin people's lives. "

Mr. Medlicott drew himself up, he was not quite so tall as the Russian, but of no mean height, and his intense, ascetic face, emaciated to extreme leanness, now reddened with passion, while the veins stood out upon his high, narrow forehead. He was always very irritable when crossed, and his obstinate nature was strongly combative.

"You forget, sir, " he said angrily, "you are insulting my honor. "

"Not the least in the world—you do not understand the point, " Count Roumovski returned calmly. "Listen for a minute—and I will explain. If Miss Rawson were already your wife I should be, and you would have the right to try and kill me, did your calling permit of that satisfaction of gentlemen, because there is a psychological and physiological reason involved in that case, producing the instinct in man which he is not perhaps conscious of, that he wishes to be sure his wife's legitimate offspring are his own—out of this instinct, civilization has built up the idea of a man's honor—which you can see has a basic principle of sense and justice. "

Mr. Medlicott with difficulty restrained himself from interrupting and the Russian went on.

"The situation of betrothed is altogether different: in it there have merely been promises exchanged, promises, for the most part, which no man or woman can honestly engage with any certainty to keep, because feeling toward the other is not within his or her control— both are promising upon a sentiment, not a reality. "

"I totally disagree with you, " Eustace Medlicott answered angrily, "when men and women make promises to one another they should have wills strong enough to keep them. "

"For what sensible reason? " Count Roumovski asked. "In a case where the happiness of both is involved, and where no damage has been incurred by either—"

Mr. Medlicott clasped his hands convulsively but he did not reply—so the Russian went on:

"Surely, you must see that a woman should be free to marry—that is, to give herself and her power to become a mother where she loves—not to be forced to bestow these sacred gifts when her spirit is unwilling—just because she has made the initial mistake of affiancing herself to a man, often through others' influence, who she discovers afterward is distasteful to her. Cannot you realize that it is wise for himself as well as for her that this man release her, before a life of long misery begins for them both? "

Mr. Medlicott never analyzed reasons, and never listened to other people's logic, and if he had any of his own he was too angry to use it. He was simply conscious now that a foreigner had insulted him and appeared to have stolen the affections of his betrothed, and his sacred calling precluded all physical retaliation—which, at the moment, was the only kind that would have given him any satisfaction. He prepared to stalk furiously from the room after he should receive an answer to an all-important question.

"The whole thing is disgraceful, " he said, "and I shall inform Miss Rawson's uncle and aunt of your highly insulting words to me, that they may guard her from further importunity upon your part. But I should like to know, in fairness, how far you are stating you have been able to persuade my fiancee to agree to your view? "

"I am sorry you should have become so heated and angry, " Count Roumovski returned, "because it stops all sensible discussion. I deeply regret having been forced to inflict pain upon you, but if you would give yourself time to think calmly you would see that, however unfortunate the fact may be for you of Miss Rawson's affections having become fixed on me—these things are no one's fault and beyond human control—Miss Rawson has left the breaking off of her engagement to you in my hands, and has decided that she desires to marry me, as I desire to marry her, as soon as she is free. "

"I refuse to listen to another word, " Mr. Medlicott flashed, "and I warn you, sir, that I will give no such freedom at your bidding—on the contrary, I shall have my marriage with Miss Rawson solemnized immediately, and try, if there is a word of truth in your preposterous assertion that she loves you, to bring her back to a proper sense of her duty to me and to God, repressing her earthly longings by discipline and self-denial, the only true methods for the saving of her soul. And I and her natural guardians, her uncle and her aunt, will take care that you never see her again. "

Count Roumovski raised his eyebrows once more and prepared to light a cigar.

"It is a pity you will not discuss this peacefully, sir, " he said, "or apparently even think about it yourself with common sense. If you would do so, you would begin by asking yourself what God gave certain human beings certain attributes for, " he blew a few whiffs of smoke, "whether to be wasted and crushed out by the intolerance of others, —or whether to be tended and grow to the highest, as flowers grow with light and air and water. "

"What has that got to do with the case? " asked Mr. Medlicott, tapping his foot uneasily.

"Everything, " went on the Russian, mildly, "you, I believe, are a priest, and therefore should be better able to expound your Deity's meaning than I, a layman—but you have evidently not the same point of view—mine is always to look at the facts of a case denuded of prejudice—because the truth is the thing to aim at—"

"You would suggest that I am not aiming at the truth, " the clergyman interrupted, trembling now with anger, so that he fiercely grasped the back of a high chair, "your words are preposterous, sir. "

"Not at all, " Count Roumovski continued. "Look frankly at things; you have just announced that you would constitute yourself judge of what is for Miss Rawson's salvation. "

"Leave her name out, I insist, " the other put in hotly.

"To be concrete, unfortunately, I cannot do so, " the Russian said. "I must speak of this lady we are both interested in—pray, try to listen to me calmly, sir, for we are here for the settling of a matter which concerns the happiness of our three lives. "

"I do not admit for a moment that you have the right to speak at all, " Mr. Medlicott returned, but his adversary went on quietly.

"You must have remarked that Miss Rawson possesses beauty of form, sweet and tender flesh, soft coloring, and a look of health and warmth and life. All these charms tend to create in man a passionate physical love. That is cause and effect. For the sake of the present argument we will, for the moment, leave out all more important questions of the soul and things mental and spiritual. Well, who gave her these attributes? Did you or I—or even her parents, consciously? Or did the Supreme Being, whom you call God, endow her so? Admitted that He did—have you, then, or anyone else, the right to crush out the result of His endowment in a woman; crush her joy of them, force her into a life where their possession is looked upon as a temptation? Seek to marry her— remember that marriage physically means being certainly actuated to do so by their attraction—and yet believing that you sin each time you allow them to influence you. " Count Roumovski's level voice took on a note of deep emotion and his blue eyes gleamed. "Why, the degradation is horrible to think of, sir, if you will face the truth—and this is the fate to which you would condemn this young and tender girl for your own selfishness, knowing she does not love you. "

Eustace Medlicott walked up and down rapidly for a moment; he then picked up a book and threw it aside again in agitation. He was very pale now.

"I refuse to have the woman I have decided to marry snatched from me by any of your sophistries, " he said breathlessly. "I am better able than you to save her soul, and she owes me honor and obedience—it is most unseemly to even mention the aspects you have done in a bond which is a sacrament of holy church and should be only approached in a spiritual frame of mind, not a carnal one. "

"You are talking pure nonsense, sir, " returned Count Roumovski sternly. "If that were the case the wording of your English marriage service would be different. First and foremost, marriage is a contract between two people to live together in union of body and to procreate children, which is the law of God and nature. Men added arrangement and endowment of property, and the church added spiritual sacrament. But God and nature invented the vital thing. If it were not so, it would have been possible for the spiritually minded, of which company you infer yourself to be, to live with a woman on terms of brother and sister, and never let the senses speak at all. There would then have been no necessity for the ceremony of marriage for priests with your views. "

Eustace Medlicott shook with passion and emotion as he answered furiously: "You would turn the question into one of whether a priest should marry or not. It is a question which has agitated me all my life, and which I have only lately been able to come to a conclusion upon. I refuse to let you disturb me in it. "

"I had not thought of doing so, " Count Roumovski returned tranquilly. "You and your views and your destiny do not interest me, I must own, except in so far as they interfere with myself and the woman I love. You have proved yourself to be just a warped atom of the great creation, incapable of anything but ignoble narrowness. You cannot even examine your own emotions honestly and probe their meaning or you would realize no man should marry, be he priest or layman, if he looks upon the joys of physical love as base and his succumbing to them a proof of the power of the beast in himself. Because he then lives under continual degradation of soul by acting against his conscience. "

Mr. Medlicott was now silent, almost choking with perturbation. So Count Roumovski went on:

"The wise man faces the facts of nature. Looks straight to find God's meaning in them, and then tries to exalt and ennoble them to their loftiest good. He does not, in his puny impotence, quarrel with the all-powerful Creator and try to stamp out that with which He thought fit to endow human beings. "

"Your words convey a flagrant denial of original sin, and I cannot listen to such an argument, " Mr. Medlicott flashed, his anger now at white heat. "You would do away with a whole principle of the Christian religion. "

"No; I would only do away with a faulty interpretation which man grafted upon it, " Count Roumovski answered.

Then the two men glared straight into each other's eyes for a moment, and Eustace Medlicott quailed beneath the magnetic force of the Russian's blue ones—he turned away abruptly. He was too intolerant of character and too disturbed now to permit himself to hear more of these reasonings. He could but resort to protest and let his wrath rise to assist him.

"It cannot benefit either Miss Rawson or ourselves to continue this unseemly controversy over her, " he said in a raucous voice. "I have told you I will give no freedom upon your request—and I have warned you of my action. Now I shall go, " and he took three steps toward the door.

But Count Roumovski's next words arrested him a moment; his tone was no longer one of suave, detached calmness, but sharp and decisive, and his bearing was instinct with strength and determination.

"Since we are coming to warnings, " he said, "we drop the velvet glove. The discourtesy to a lady conveyed in your words obliges me to use my own way without further consulting you for assisting her wishes. I will again thank you for coming up here and will have the honor to wish you goodnight. " With which he opened the door politely and bowed his visitor out.

And when he was alone Count Roumovski sat down by the open window and puffed his cigar meditatively for some minutes, smiling quietly to himself as he mused:

"Poor, stupid fellow! If people could only be honest enough with themselves to have a sensible point of view! It is all so simple if they would get down to the reason of things without all this false sentiment. Of what use to chain the body of a woman to one man if her spirit is with another? Of what use to talk of offended honor with high-sounding words when, if one were truthful, one would own it was offended vanity? Of what use for this narrow, foolish clergyman to protest and bombast and rave, underneath he is actuated by mostly human motives in his desire to marry my Stella? When will the world learn to be natural and see the truth? Love of the soul is the divine part of the business, but it cannot exist without love of the body. As well ask a man to live upon bread without water. "

Then he moved to his writing table and composed rapidly a letter to his beloved in which he recounted to her the result of the interview and the threats of her late fiance, and the humor in which he had quitted the room, and from that she might judge of what she must reasonably expect. He advised her, as he was unaware of how far the English authority of a guardian might go, to feign some fatigue and keep her room next day and on no account whatever to be persuaded to leave Rome or the hotel. He told her that in the morning he would endeavor to see her uncle and aunt, but if they refused this interview, he would write and ask formally for her hand, and if his request were treated with scorn, then she must be prepared to slip away with him to the Excelsior Hotel and be consigned to the care of the Princess Urazov, his sister, who would have arrived from Paris. The business part of the epistle over, he allowed himself half a page of love sentences—which caused Miss Rawson exquisite delight when she read them some moments later.

She had not gone to bed directly, she was too excited and full of new emotions to be thinking of sleep, and when she heard Ivan's gentle tap at her door she crept to it and whispered without opening it:

"Who is there? "

A low voice answered: "Une lettre pour mademoiselle. " And the epistle was slipped into the little box for letters on the door. She went back to her wide window and looked out on the darkness after she had read it. She saw there would be trouble ahead, she knew Eustace Medlicott's obstinate spirit very well, and also the rigid convention of Aunt Caroline—but to what lengths they would go she formulated no guess.

It all seemed so secure and happy and calm now with such a man to lean upon as Sasha Roumovski. Nothing need ruffle or frighten her ever any more. And then she read the love sentences again and thrilled and quivered there in the warm, soft night. Sasha Roumovski's influence over her had grown so strong that not a questioning speculation as to the step she meant to take any longer entered her head. She felt she knew at last what love's meaning truly was, and nothing else mattered in the world—which, indeed, was the truth!

Meanwhile, the Reverend Eustace Medlicott, burning with fury, had stalked to his room, and there tried to think of what he had better do.

He feared it was too late to communicate with Canon and Mrs. Ebley—they would have retired to bed, and Stella, also. Here his thoughts were brought up with violent suddenness. Was she quite safe? Heavens above! and he turned quite cold—foreigners might be capable of any outrage—but presently he dismissed this fear. People always locked their doors in hotels, and Stella, though she had apparently shown herself sadly unworthy of his regard, was a thoroughly well brought-up young woman, and would not be likely to bandy words in the night with any young man. But on the morrow he would insist upon their all leaving the hotel and Rome itself—no more chances of her communicating with this hateful Russian count should be risked.

As the Ebley party had only arrived three days ago in the city, it was clearly impossible that the affair could have gone far, and as he had heard of their sightseeing and knew Mrs. Ebley would be extremely unlikely to allow Stella out of her sight in any case, he could not imagine how his fiancee and the Russian could have found a chance to speak—and even a foreigner could not persuade a woman into this course of action in half an hour's talk at the Embassy! The whole thing must be the ravings of a madman, nothing more, and Stella herself would be the first to explain that point on the morrow.

But even this comforting thought could not quite calm him—there remained disquieting recollections of certain forcible arguments he had been obliged to listen to against his will which had hit some part of his inner consciousness usually impregnably protected by his self-conceit. And it was an hour or two before he was able to drink his barley water and retire to rest, which he felt he badly needed after his long journey and uncomfortably exciting evening.

CHAPTER VI

The sun was blazing gloriously next day, the whole air was full of freshness and spring and youth. An ideal one for lovers, and not at all the atmosphere for anger and strife. But these facts did not enter into the consideration of three of the people, at least, connected with our little comedy.

Eustace Medlicott woke more full of wrath than he had been the night before, and, the moment he was dressed, proceeded to make havoc with the peace of the Reverend Canon and Mrs. Ebley. He sent up an urgent summons that they would see him immediately. Having no sitting-room, he suggested the reading-room, which would be empty at this hour.

The Aunt Caroline had experienced some misgivings herself at the Embassy about her niece's absence with the foreign count, who had risen to this distinctive appellation in her mind from "that dreadful man, " but she had felt it more prudent not to comment upon her apprehensions to her niece. Eustace evidently had discovered further cause of resentment and feminine curiosity assisted her to dress with greater rapidity than usual.

The pair entered the room with grave faces and took two uncomfortable chairs.

The Reverend Mr. Medlicott remained standing, and soon, from his commanding position, let them hear his version of the hated foreigner's communications. They were duly horrified and surprised and then Mrs. Ebley bridled a little—after all, it was the behavior of her own niece upon which aspersion was being cast.

"I am certain, Eustace, the man must be mad—I assure you, Stella has not been for an instant absent from me, except yesterday morning she went to the Thermes Museum with Martha, whom you know has proved by twenty-five years of faithful service that she can be completely trusted, therefore the girl cannot have had any opportunity of conversing with this stranger until last night. It would be only fair to question her first—"

"My wife is quite right, " Canon Ebley agreed. "We should listen to no more until Stella is here to defend herself. Let us send a message for her to descend at once. "

He went and rang the bell as he spoke, and the summons to Miss Rawson was dispatched. Then the three somewhat uncomfortably tried to exchange platitudes upon indifferent subjects until the waiter returned.

Mademoiselle was very fatigued and was not yet up! Such an unheard of thing petrified them all with astonishment. Stella to be still in bed, at half past nine in the morning! The child must be ill! — or it was distinct rebellion. Mrs. Ebley prepared to go and investigate matters when another waiter entered with a note for Canon Ebley, and stood aside to receive the answer.

"Dear, dear! " said that gentleman to his wife, "I have not my glasses with me, I came down in such a hurry. Will you read it to me? "

But Mrs. Ebley was in a like plight, so they were obliged to enlist the services of Eustace Medlicott.

He knew the writing directly he glanced at it and every move of his body stiffened with renewed anger. And it is to be feared he said to himself, "it is from that cursed man. "

He read it aloud, and it was the briefest and most courteous note asking for the honor of an interview at whatever time would be most agreeable to Canon Ebley. The nature of the business to be discussed at it was not stated.

"I strongly advise you not to see the scoundrel, " Mr. Medlicott said vehemently. "It is far better that we should all leave Rome immediately and avoid any chance of scandal. "

"Before we can decide anything, " Mrs. Ebley said decisively, "I must speak with my niece. If she is quite ignorant of this foreigner's ravings, then there will be no necessity to alter our trip—we can merely move to another hotel. The whole thing is most unpleasant and irritating and has quite upset me. "

Stella, upstairs in her cosy bed, had meanwhile received another note from her lover. Full of tenderness and encouragement, it made her feel as bold as a young lioness and ready to brave any attack. That her aunt had not been to see why she was not dressed already was filling her with surprise, and after the waiter had brought the message she guessed the reason why.

A firm tap to the door presently and her Aunt Caroline's voice saying sternly. "It is I, Stella, please let me in at once. "

Miss Rawson got out of bed, unlocked the door and bounded back again, and a figure of dignified displeasure sailed into the room.

"Are you ill, my dear? " Mrs. Ebley asked, in a stern voice. "It is otherwise very strange that you should not be dressed at this hour—it is a quarter to ten o'clock. "

"No, I am not exactly ill, Aunt Caroline, " Stella answered gently, "but I was very tired, and as I was making up my mind what I should say in my letter to Eustace to break off my engagement—I preferred not to come down until I had done so. "

The Aunt Caroline could not believe her ears. She was obliged to sit down. Her emotion made her knees tremble. It was true then—something had been going on under her very eyes and she had not perceived it—the deceit and perfidy of human nature had always been a shock to her—

"You wish to break your engagement, Stella, " she said, as soon as she could steady her voice. "But you cannot possibly do so scandalous a thing—and for what reason, pray? "

"I find I do not love Eustace, " Stella answered calmly, although her heart now began to beat rapidly. "I know I never have loved him; it was only because I thought it would please you and Uncle Erasmus that I ever became engaged to him, and now that I know what love is—I mean now that the time is getting nearer, I feel that I cannot go through with it. "

"There is something underneath all this, Stella, " Mrs. Ebley said icily. "You cannot deceive me. You have been led astray, girl—it is wiser to confess at once and I will try to pardon you. "

Stella's spirit rose—she raised her head proudly, then she remembered her lover's counsel to have no arguments whatsoever, and so she curbed her heated words and continued gently:

"I have not been led astray, Aunt Caroline, and there is nothing to pardon. I am twenty-one years old now and surely can judge for myself whether or no I wish to marry a man—and I have decided I do not intend to marry Eustace Medlicott. I almost feel I detest him. "

Mrs. Ebley was petrified with anger and astonishment.

"I am sorry to tell you I cannot believe you, Stella, " she said, "your fiance had a most unpleasant shock last night. The foreign person, Count Roumovski, who was presented to us at the Embassy, insulted him greatly, and told him that you had agreed to marry him as soon as Eustace should set you free! I almost blush to repeat to you this shocking story which we had considered the ravings of a madman, but the time has come when we must have some plain speaking. "

"It has indeed, " Stella agreed, her wrath rising, then went on respectfully, "but I must refuse to discuss anything about Count Roumovski at present. Please believe me that I do not wish to annoy you, dear Aunt Caroline. I only wish to do what is right, and I know it is right to break off my engagement with Eustace Medlicott. "

Mrs. Ebley felt her anger augmenting to boiling point, but nothing, she could say had any effect upon her niece, who remained extremely respectful and gentle, but perfectly firm. Mrs. Ebley could not get her to tell her anything about her acquaintance with this dreadful foreigner. She became silent after she had refused point blank to discuss him. At last the baffled and exasperated older lady got up and fired her last shot.

"Words cannot express my pain and disgust at your conduct, Stella, " she said. "Putting aside all the awful suspicions I have about this Russian, you will lay up for yourself a lifelong regret in outraging all decency by refusing to marry that good and pure young clergyman, Eustace Medlicott. "

"I have done nothing wrong, Aunt Caroline, please do not go away angry with me, " Stella pleaded. "When Count Roumovski asks Uncle Erasmus' and your consent to his marrying me—then I will tell you everything about him, —but now I do not wish to. Please forgive me for causing you pain—we shall all be very happy soon, and surely I have a right to my life like any other person. "

Mrs. Ebley would not bandy further words; their points of view were too different.

"I regret that I am obliged to request you to keep your room and have no communication with anyone whatever until I can consult with your uncle and Eustace as to what is the best thing to do with you. That we shall leave Rome immediately you may be prepared for. "

Stella here burst into tears. She had an affection for her aunt, who had always been kind to her in a hard, cold way, and she was deeply grieved at their estrangement, but there were forces in life which she knew now mattered more than any aunts in the world.

Mrs. Ebley did not relent at the sound of the sobbing, but left the room, closing the door firmly after her. And a few minutes afterward Martha was let in by the chambermaid without knocking and sat down grimly by the window and began to knit.

Then Stella's tears turned to resentment. To be insulted so! To have a servant sent to watch her was more than she would bear. But as she turned in bed she felt her lover's note touch her and like a magic wand a thrill of comfort rushed through her. After all, he would settle things for her—and meanwhile she would close her eyes and pretend to sleep. So with her precious love letter clasped tight in her hand under the clothes she turned her face to the wall and shut her eyes.

Meanwhile, Canon Ebley and the Reverend Eustace Medlicott were spending a very disagreeable time in the reading-room. Relieved of Mrs. Ebley's presence, Eustace had recounted more fully the interview he had had with Sasha Roumovski the night before. He was not a very accurate person and apt to color everything with his own prejudice, so Canon Ebley did not obtain a very clear idea of the Russian's arguments. They seemed to him to be very unorthodox and carnal and reprehensible from all points. But it was evident they were dealing with a clever and dangerous character and Stella must be rescued from such a person's influence and married off to her lawful fiance at once.

"We could have the ceremony here, Eustace, in three weeks' time, or we could go back to England immediately, for until our niece is your wife I am sure her aunt and myself will not feel easy about her. "

"Nor I either, " Mr. Medlicott returned, and at that moment the Aunt Caroline entered the room and gradually disclosed the awful truth she had arrived at from Miss Rawson's admissions.

"That dreadful foreigner must be told at once we refuse to have any communication with him and Stella shall be kept locked in her room until we can leave Rome, " Mrs. Ebley said sternly. "I could not have believed my own sister's child could have behaved so disgracefully. "

"Dear, dear, " said Canon Ebley, "but we must get at the facts of when she has been able to see this Russian. It is impossible that the present state of things could have arisen from merely last night at the Embassy. "

At this stage of the proceedings, it being a public room, Count Roumovski entered it serenely and, coming toward the group, made a stiff bow to each in turn.

"I believe you have received my letter, sir, " he said, addressing Canon Ebley, "but, as I have had no reply, I ventured to present myself without further delay—"

"We do not wish for any communication from you, " Eustace Medlicott hastened to announce before either of the others could speak. "I have informed Canon and Mrs. Ebley of your disgraceful conduct and that is sufficient. We shall discuss nothing further. "

"I was not addressing you, sir, " Count Roumovski returned mildly. "My business with you terminated last night. " And he turned his shoulders to the irate junior chaplain and looked Canon Ebley straight in the face. "I am here to ask for the hand of your niece, Miss Rawson, as she is now free from other engagements, and with her full consent I desire to make her my wife. "

"Come, Erasmus, " Mrs. Ebley said with icy dignity. "Let us go up to our apartment and if this person annoys us further we can complain to the manager of the hotel, " then, with an annihilating glance, she took her husband's arm and drew him toward the door.

"As you will, madame, " and the Russian gentleman bowed with respectful serenity. "It would have been more sensible to have taken my request otherwise, but it is, after all, quite immaterial. I will wish you a good-day, " and he bowed again as Canon Ebley and his outraged spouse sailed from the room—and, with an exclamation of suppressed fury, Eustace Medlicott followed in their wake.

Then Count Roumovski laughed softly to himself and, sitting down at a writing-table, wrote a letter to his beloved. His whole plan of life was simple and direct. He had done what he considered was necessary in the affair, he had behaved with perfect openness and honor in his demand, and if these people could not see the thing from a common sense point of view, they were no longer to be considered. He would take the law into his own hands.

When he had finished his note he went straight up in the lift to the corridor where Stella's room was and there saw in the distance her raging and discomfited late betrothed evidently keeping watch and ward. Count Roumovski did not hesitate a second; he advanced to the door and knocked firmly on the panel, slipping his letter through the little slide for such things before Mr. Medlicott could bound forward and prevent him.

"A letter for you, mademoiselle, from me, Sasha Roumovski, " he said in French in a loud enough voice for the occupant of the room to hear, and then he stood still for a second, as both men heard Stella jump from her bed and rush to the door to take the missive before Martha from the place at the window could intercept it.

"Do not dare to touch that, Martha, " they heard her voice say haughtily, and then she called out, "Sasha, I have it safe and I will do exactly as you direct. "

Count Roumovski looked at Eustace Medlicott, who stood as a spread-eagle in front of the door—and then, smiling, went calmly on his way.

The Reverend Mr. Medlicott shook with burning rage. He was being made to look ridiculous and he was absolutely impotent to retaliate in any way. He would bring scandal upon them all if waiters and other guests saw him guarding Miss Rawson's actual door, and he could not sit outside like a valet; the whole thing was unspeakably maddening, and murderous thoughts flooded his brain.

The Point of View

"Give me that letter this minute, Stella, " he said in an almost inarticulate voice through the keyhole, he was so shaken with passion. "Open the door and let Martha hand it to me. You are disgracing us all. "

"It is you who are doing that, Eustace, " Stella said from beyond the panel, lifting the slide that her voice might be heard distinctly. "You have no authority over me at all. I told Aunt Caroline I did not intend to continue my engagement with you—but even if I had not decided to break it off, this conduct of yours would now be sufficient reason. How dare you all treat me as though I were a naughty child or insane! "

"Because you are both, " Mr. Medlicott returned, "and must be controlled and compelled into a proper behavior. "

Stella was silent—she would not be so undignified as to parley further. She got back into bed, taking not the slightest notice of the maid, and then proceeded to read her letter.

Her lover had explained in it the situation and advised her to dress at once, and then if menaced in any way to ring the bell. Ivan would be waiting outside to obey her slightest orders, and to warn his master if any fresh moves were made, so that when the waiter or chambermaid came in answer to her summons she might be sure of extra help at hand. Then she was to walk out and down into the hall, where he, Sasha, would be watching for her and ready to take her to the Excelsior Hotel, where that same evening would arrive the Princess Urazov. "But if they do not molest you, dearest, " he wrote, "do not leave your room until seven o'clock, because I wish my sister to be in the hall ready to receive you that your family can see that I only desire to do everything right. "

And as she finished reading, Stella got up and told Martha to prepare her things.

"I have no orders from Mrs. Ebley for that, Miss Stella, " the woman answered sullenly. "I do wonder what has come over everybody. I never was in such an uncomfortable position in my life. "

Stella made no answer, but proceeded to dress herself, and then sat down to read again the letters she had received in the last twenty-four hours.

If her family, who knew her, could treat her in this abominable way, when she had committed no fault except the very human one of desiring to be the arbiter of her own fate, she surely owed no further obedience to them. So she waited calmly for a fresh turn of events.

Her luncheon was brought up on a tray by the waiter, and some for Martha also, and the two ate in silence, until Stella suddenly burst into a merry peal of laughter, it was so grotesquely comic! A grown up English girl in these days locked in her room with a dragon duenna gaoler!

"Martha, isn't it too funny, the whole thing! " she said, between her gurgles. "Can't you laugh, you old goose! and to think how sorry you will be, you were so horrid, when I am gone, because, of course, you know you cannot keep me once I make up my mind to go. "

"Mrs. Ebley said I was to have no conversation with you, Miss, " Martha said, glumly, at which Stella laughed afresh.

Meanwhile Count Roumovski had made all arrangements at the Excelsior Hotel, and after lunch sat quietly in the hall awaiting his beloved. Mrs. Ebley had felt too upset to go down to the restaurant, so the two clergymen were there alone, and glanced wrathfully at the imperturbable face of Count Roumovski seated at his usual table, with his air of detached aloofness and perfect calm. They, on the contrary, were so boiling with rage that they knew not what they ate.

After lunch it had been decided that the party should leave the Grand and take the five o'clock train to Florence, and their preparations were made.

Mrs. Ebley had herself been laboriously packing so as not to take Martha from her post, and orders were whispered to that faithful Abigail through Stella's letter slide to pack Miss Rawson's things at once.

Stella watched these preparations serenely, and gave Martha directions as to what to put on the top. Then when all was finished and she had donned her hat, she rang the electric bell for the waiter, and when he knocked at the door she calmly bade him enter, which, of course, he was able to do with his key, and she told him in French, which Martha did not understand, to send the porters there immediately, and have her luggage consigned to the care of the servant who would be waiting in the passage. This person would give orders for its destination. The waiter bowed obsequiously. Had he not been already heavily tipped by this intelligent Ivan, and instructed instantly to obey the orders of mademoiselle? "

"It is much better I am before them, " Stella thought to herself, while Martha looked on in rageful bafflement.

"The porters will come up and take the trunks outside, Martha, " Miss Rawson said. "You can give them what orders aunt told you to. "

Such was her supreme confidence in the methods of her lover that she felt sure once Ivan was apprised of the fact by the waiter that the trunks would be consigned to him it would not matter what Martha said to the porters! So she calmly sat down by the window and folded her hands, while the elderly maid fumed with the uncertainty of what she ought to do. And in a few moments the men appeared, and smilingly seemed to understand the gestures and English orders of Martha to take the trunks to the door of Madam Ebley, number 325, round the corner of the passage and on the opposite side.

They nodded their heads wisely and carried the box out, shutting the door after them, and then there was silence for a while; and Stella half-dozed in her chair, it was so warm and peaceful by the window and she had had so little sleep in the night.

An hour passed, and at four o'clock the Aunt Caroline appeared. Her face was grim. Had Stella been an outcast in deed and word she could not have looked more disdainful.

"You must come down with me now, Stella, " she said, "we are ready to go to the station. I will remain with you here until Martha gets her hat. "

Stella rose to her feet and before the astonished lady could speak more, she had swiftly passed her and gained the door, which she threw open, and, like a fawn, rushed down the passage toward the staircase entrance side of the hotel, and by the time her slowly moving aunt had emerged from the room she had turned the corner and was out of sight.

Fortunately, she met no one on the stairs except one astonished page, and arrived in the outer corridor breathless with excitement and emotion.

Count Roumovski saw her through the door of the hall, and hastened to meet her.

"There is not a moment to be lost, " she said, as he got to her side.

"Go to the place you went before under the trees, " he whispered hurriedly in return. "The automobile is there, and I will follow presently. " So she went.

Her knees would hardly support her, she trembled so, until she was safe in the big blue motor, which moved off at once. For an awful moment a hideous sense of terror overcame her, making her cold. What lay in front of her? What new fate? —and then joy and life came back. She was going to freedom and love-away from Exminster and dreary duties—away from Eustace Medlicott, for ever! For, of course, her uncle and aunt would come round in time, and they could be happy again with her some day.

When Mrs. Ebley had collected her scattered senses and followed down the passage only to find Stella out of sight, she was obliged to retrace her steps and rejoin her husband and Mr. Medlicott, who were awaiting her at the lift on the other side, the restaurant end, which was the one they were accustomed to descend by.

"She ran away from me, Erasmus! " the agitated lady cried, "passed me without a word, and I suppose has gone down the stairs—if we hasten in the lift we shall catch her yet. "

But as they frantically rang the bell and the lift boy did not come, Eustace Medlicott, with a most unsaintly exclamation, hastened off by that staircase and arrived in the hall to see the hated Russian calmly smoking his cigarette and reading an English paper.

He advanced upon him regardless of the numbers of people beginning to assemble for tea.

"What have you done with Miss Rawson? " he asked furiously. "She has this moment run away from her aunt. "

"I have nothing to converse with you about, " Count Roumovski returned, with mild surprise. "And, as I see it is four o'clock, I must wish you a good-day, as I have an appointment, " with which he rose quietly before the other could prevent him, and crossed the broad path of carpet which separates the groups of chairs, and there was seen to enter into earnest conversation with a Russian- looking individual who had just entered.

The Reverend Mr. Medlicott was nonplussed, and hurried into the front vestibule, where he made rapid inquiries of the hall-porter.

Yes—the young lady, he believed, had walked out of the hotel not two minutes before. Monsieur would overtake her certainly, if he hastened. And the frantic young man rushed from the door, through the porte cochere, and so to the street, but all he saw in the far distance was a retreating large, blue automobile—and this conveyed among all the rest of the traffic no impression whatever.

To search for Stella was hopeless; the only thing to do was to return to the Ebleys, and with them go to the Embassy. There they could, perhaps, get advice and help how to communicate with the police.

But what an ignominious position for a Bishop's junior chaplain to be placed in, a humiliation in every way!

CHAPTER VII

When Stella found the automobile drawing up at a strange hotel's doors her tremors broke out afresh, until she saw the face of Ivan, who, with the porter, came forward to meet her, saying respectfully in French, would mademoiselle be pleased to mount directly to the rooms reserved for the Princess Urazov? And soon, without anyone questioning her, she found herself being taken up in the lift, and finally ushered into a charming sitting-room full of flowers.

Here she sat down and trembled again. The wildest excitement filled her veins. Would Sasha never come! She could not sit still, she walked from bouquet to bouquet of roses and carnations, sniffing the scent, and at last subsided into a big armchair, as the waiters brought in some tea.

He thought of everything for her, then—her lover. But oh, why did he not come!

She had finished her tea and had begun her restless pacing again, when, with a gentle tap, the door opened, and Count Roumovski appeared.

"Sasha! " she cried, and advanced toward him like a frightened child.

His usually calm blue eyes were blazing with some emotion which disturbed her greatly, she knew not why, and his voice seemed to have taken a tone of extra deepness, as he said:

"Stella! My little star! And so you are really here—and my own! "

He put his strong hands down and held on to the back of a chair, and simple as she was she knew very well that otherwise he would have taken her into his arms, which was where she was longing to be, if she had known.

"Yes, I have come, " she whispered, "I have left them all—for you. Oh! when will your sister be here? "

"Not until six o'clock, darling, " he answered, while his eyes melted upon her with passionate love. "There is an hour yet to wait. I had

64

hoped you would not have been forced to leave your aunt's care until then. "

"Oh! I am delighted to have come away, " Stella answered, regaining some of her composure. "I was shut into my room and watched by a servant. It was awful! But do—you know what has happened now? since I left? Are they tearing about after me, or what? "

Count Roumovski still held on to the back of the chair, and his voice was still deep, as he said:

"I believe they have gone to your Embassy in a band—and much good may they get there. You are of age, you see. Besides, I have taken care that no one at the Grand Hotel knows where we have gone, and it will take them quite an hour or two to telephone about and find out—and by that time my sister will have arrived, and we can defy them. "

"Yes, " said Stella, and then, nervously, "won't you have some tea? "

He sat down, still constrainedly and clasped his hands, and womanlike, when she saw his agitation, her own lessened, and she assumed command, while she asked almost archly if he took cream and sugar.

He liked neither, he said, and with the air of a little hostess she handed him the cup. Then she smiled softly and stood quite near him.

He drew himself together and his face looked almost stern as he took the tea, and over Stella there crept a chill—and the gay little speech that had been bubbling to her lips died there, and a silence fell upon them for a few moments. Then he put down his cup and crossed to the stiff sofa where she was, and sat down beside her.

"Sweetheart, " he said, looking deeply into her eyes, "it is a colossal temptation, you know, to me to make love to you. But I am not going to permit myself that happiness yet. I want to tell you all about what we shall do presently, and see if it pleases you. " He did not even take her hand, and Stella felt rather aggrieved and wounded. "I propose that as soon as the formalities can be got through, and the wedding can take place, that we go straight to Paris—because you will want to get all kinds of clothes. And it will be such a delight to me to give you everything you wish for. "

Stella smiled shyly. It seemed suddenly to bring realities of things before her with keen force. He would have the right to give her everything in the world—this man whom she did not really know, but whom she felt she loved very much. She clasped her hands and a thrill ran through her. What, what did it all mean? The idea of her marriage with Eustace Medlicott had always appeared as an ugly vision, an end to everything, a curtain which was yet drawn over a view which could only be all dusk and gray shadows, and which she would rather not contemplate. But now the thought of going away and beginning a new existence with Sasha Roumovski was something so glorious and delicious that she quivered with joy at any reference to it.

Her little movement and the clasping of her hands affected him profoundly. He, too, quivered, but with the stern effort to control himself. It was part of his code of honor. Not the slightest advantage must be taken of the situation while Stella was alone and unchaperoned, although the very fact of their propinquity and the knowledge of their solitude were extremely exciting to him, who knew the meaning of every emotion. He drew a little away from her, and said in a voice that sounded cold:

"I have seen the consul this afternoon. It will take three weeks, I am afraid, before we can be legally married here in Rome. It seems an eternity to me. "

"Yes, " agreed Stella, and suddenly looked down. She wished intensely that he would caress her a little—although she was unaware of the desire. She wondered vaguely—was it then very wicked to make love, since Sasha, too, like Eustace, seemed as if he were resisting something with all his strength? And unconsciously she pouted her red underlip, and Count Roumovski moved convulsively.

"My sister's room is next to this, " he said, "and yours is beyond. I have had only roses put there, because you are like a sweet June rose. "

"Am I? " said Miss Rawson, and raised her head. She had grown extremely excited and disappointed, and, she knew not what, only that she did not like this new lover of hers to be sitting there constrained and aloof, talking in a stiff voice unlike his usual easy grace. It was perfectly ridiculous to have run away with some one with whom she was passionately in love, if he were going to remain as cold as ice!

She got up and took a rose from a vase and fastened it in her dress. The whole movement and action had the unconscious coquetry of a woman's methods to gain her end. Totally unaccustomed as Stella was to all artifices, instinct was her teacher.

Sasha Roumovski rose suddenly.

"Come and sit here beside me again, heart of mine, " he commanded with imperious love, and indicated the stiff Louis XIV sofa. "I must explain everything to you, it would seem. "

Stella had never heard this tone in his voice before; it caused her strange delight, and she shyly took her seat at one end of the sofa, and then, as he flung himself down beside her, she looked up at him.

"What must you explain? " she asked.

"First, that I love you madly, that it is sickening temptation to be with you now every instant without holding you in my arms, " and his voice trembled, while his blue eyes glowed. "That I do not know how to resist the wild passion which is overcoming me. I want to kiss you so terribly, more than I have ever wanted anything in my life. "

"We-ll? " said Stella, with a quiver of exquisite joy. "And—" she had almost spoken her thought of, "Why do you not do so, then? " — but the burning passion she read in his made her drop her eyes. This was too much for him. He understood perfectly, and, with a little cry, he drew her to him, and his lips had almost touched her red, young, pouting lips when he suddenly controlled himself and put her from him.

"No, sweetheart, " he said hoarsely, "you would never respect me any more if I took advantage of your tenderness now. As soon—as soon as I really may, I will teach you every shade of love and its meanings. I will kiss those lips and unloosen that hair; I will suffocate you with caresses and make you thrill as I shall thrill until we both forget everything in the intoxication of bliss, " and he half-closed his eyes, and his face grew pale again with suppressed emotion.

"Oh, I do not understand at all, " Stella said, in a disappointed and perplexed voice. "Since we are going to be married, why would it be so very wrong for you to kiss me? I—I—" her small rueful face, with its sweet childlike irregular curves, looked almost pathetically comic, and Sasha leaned forward and covered his eyes with his hands. And then he mastered himself and laughed softly.

"Oh, you adorable one! " he said. "It is not wrong—not the least wrong. Only presently, when you do understand, you will realize how very much I loved you to-day. "

But Stella was still pouting—and got up restlessly and went to the window.

"What can they do when they get to the Embassy? " she asked. "Could they really take me back if they found me by telephoning round? "

"I do not think so—if you are past twenty-one. "

"I was twenty-one in April. I am not a bit afraid of them, but I do not want to have any row. "

"When my sister has arrived you must write to your aunt, and tell where you are and what are your intentions, then all will be finished. "

"Oh, I wish she would come, don't you? " Stella said.

"More than I can say, darling, " he answered, fervently. "You will not, I hope, find me so incomprehensible then. "

He walked about the room once or twice, and at last paused in front of her.

"Stella, " he whispered, while his eyes blazed again, "I cannot bear it, little sweetheart, to stay all alone with you here. Will you forgive me, if I leave you until Anastasia has arrived? Go and rest in your room, darling, and I will go to the station to meet her. Ivan will remain outside your door and you will be quite safe. "

But Stella put out her hands like a frightened baby.

"Oh. must you leave me? " she cried, pettishly. "You are very cruel! You make me almost wish I had not come. "

From having swum with love and passion his eyes suddenly gave forth a flash of steel, and his voice was like ice as he answered:

"If that is so, mademoiselle, it is not too late. I would not exact any unwilling sacrifice. Shall I take you back again? "

And then Stella's childishness melted and fell from her, and she became a real woman as she looked into his stern face.

"No—" she said, "I will not go back. I am sorry I was so uncontrolled, but I am nervous—and I do not know exactly what I am—Sasha, please take care of me, " and she held out her hands with a piteous gesture of asking for his protection, and moved beyond all power of further control he folded her in his arms.

"My darling, my darling! " he murmured, frantically kissing her hair. But his iron will reasserted itself in a few seconds, and while he still held her he said with more calm:

"Little star, you must never speak to me like that again, as you did just now, I mean. It was unreasonable and not kind, if you but knew! And I have a very arrogant temper, I fear, although I am nearly master of it, and shall be quite in time, I hope. We might have parted then and spoilt both our lives. Won't you believe me that I love—I adore you! " he went on tenderly. "I am madly longing to be for you the most passionate lover a woman ever had. It is only for your sake and for honor and our future happiness that I restrain myself now. You see I am not an Englishman who can accept half-measures. Do not make it impossible for me, sweet love! "

His voice was almost a sob in its deep notes of pleading, and Stella was touched.

"Oh! you are so dear and great, " she answered fondly. "I am perhaps very wicked to have tempted you. If it would be wrong for you to kiss me, which I cannot understand, it is—oh, it is because I love you like that, too! "

At this ingenuous admission, passion nearly overcame him again, and he held her so tightly it seemed as if he must crush out her very breath. Then he put her from him and walked toward the door.

"I dare not stay another second, " he said, in a strangled voice. "Ivan will guard your room, and my sister will come to you soon. Do as I tell you, beloved one, and then all will be well. "

With which he opened the door, and left her standing by the sofa quivering with a strange joy and perplexity—and some other wild emotion of which she had not dreamed.

CHAPTER VIII

It seemed an endless time the hour that she waited in her room, and then a knock came to the door, and Ivan's voice saying his master desired her presence in the sitting-room at once, and she hurriedly went there to find Count Roumovski standing by the mantelpiece looking very grave.

"Stella, " he said, "there has been an accident to the train my sister was to have arrived by—it is not serious, but she cannot be here now until the early morning perhaps—unless I send the automobile to Viterbo for her. The line is blocked by a broken- down goods train which caused the disaster, " he paused a moment, and Stella said, "Well? " rather anxiously.

"It will be impossible for us to remain here, " he continued, "because it may be that your relations, aided by the Embassy, will have traced us before then, and if they should come upon us alone together, nothing that I could say or prove could keep the situation from looking compromising, "—he now spoke with his old calm, and Stella felt her confidence reviving. He would certainly arrange what was best for them, she could rely upon that.

"What must we do then? " she asked gently, while she put her head on the sleeve of his coat.

"I will wrap you up in the fur cloak, darling, " he said, "and you must come in the automobile with me to meet Anastasia. Your family must not find you again until your are in my sister's company. We ought to start at once. "

It spoke eloquently for the impression which he had been able to create in Stella's imagination of his integrity and reliability, for the thought never entered her brain that it was a most unusual and even hazardous undertaking to start out into the night in a foreign land with a stranger she had not yet known for a week. But that was the remarkable thing about his personality; it conveyed always an atmosphere of trust and confidence.

It was not long before Miss Rawson was ready, wrapped in the long gray cloak she had worn before, and with the veil tied over her hat, and was descending in the lift alone with Ivan—her lover having gone on by the stairs.

Their departure was managed with intelligence. Stella and the servant simply walking out of the hotel and down the street to where the car waited, and then presently Count Roumovski joined them, and they started.

"Ivan will remain behind to answer any questions if the reverend clergyman and your aunt do come, " he said, when they were seated in the car in the settling sunlight. "And now, sweetheart, we can enjoy our drive. "

Stella felt deliciously excited, all the exultation of adventure thrilling her, and the joy of her lover's presence. She cared not where they were going, it was all heaven.

"We shall stop at a little restaurant for some dinner, " he said, "it will be rather bad, but we must not mind, it would not have been wise to risk any well-known place, " and soon they drew up at a small cafe on the outskirts of Rome, where there were a few people already seated at little tables under the trees. They were all Italians, and took no notice of the Russian and his lady.

It was the greatest amusement to them both, this primitive place, and to be all alone ordering their first meal together, and Sasha Roumovski exerted himself to charm and please her. He had recovered complete mastery of himself, it would seem, and his manner, while tenderly devoted, had an air of proprietorship which affected Stella exceedingly.

They spent an enchanting half hour, as gay as two children, with all the exquisite under-current of love in their talk; and then they got into the motor again.

"Let us have it open, " Count Roumovski said. "The evening drive will be divine. "

And Stella agreed.

The road to Viterbo is far from good, one of those splendid routes which lead from Rome which ought to be so perfect and in reality are a mass of ruts and pitfalls for the unwary. The jolting of the car constantly threw Stella almost into her lover's arms, who was sitting as aloof as possible. He had gradually become nearly silent, and sat there holding her hand under the rug, using the whole of his strong will to suppress his rising emotion.

The beautiful colors of the lights of evening over the Campagna; the sense of the spring time and the knowledge that she belonged to him heart and body and soul were madly intoxicating as they rushed through the air. He dared not let himself caress her gently, which he might have permitted himself to do, and he held her little hand so tightly it was almost pain to her.

As for Stella, she was profoundly in love. Her whole nature seemed to be awaking and blooming with a new grace and meaning. Her soft eyes, which glanced at him in the glowing dusk, swam with tenderness and unconscious passion, and once she let her head rest upon his shoulder, when a violent jerk threw her toward him, and at last he encircled her with his arm and there they sat trembling together, she with she knew not what, and he very well knowing, and fighting with temptation.

Thus they spent an hour in a bliss that was growing to agony for him, and then it grew perfectly dark, and the stars came out in myriads in the deep blue sky, and on in front of them the headlights of the motor made a flaming path in the night.

And all this while he had resisted his strong desires, and never even kissed her.

At last human endurance came to an end, and he said to her almost fiercely:

"Stella, my beloved one, I cannot bear this, I can no longer answer for myself. I shall settle you comfortably among the furs where you must try to sleep, and I shall go outside with the chauffeur. If I were to stay—"

And something in the tone of his voice and in his eyes made her at last have some dim, incomprehensible fear, and yet exaltation, and so she did not try to dissuade him, and soon was alone endeavoring to collect her thoughts and understand the situation.

Thus eventually they reached Viterbo, and drew up at the station door, when Count Roumovski seemed to have regained his usual calm as he helped her out with tender solicitude. The passengers, they learned, were still in the train, half a mile up the line, waiting until it was cleared to go on to Rome.

At last, after generous greasing of palms, permission was given for Count Roumovski to walk on and find his sister. And Stella was put back into the motor to await their coming.

Her heart began to beat violently. What would she be like, this future sister-in-law? She must be very fond of Sasha to have come from Paris at a moment's notice like this, to do his bidding. It seemed a long time before she heard voices, and saw in the dim light two figures advancing from the station entrance, and then Count Roumovski opened the door of the automobile, and Stella started forward to get out.

"Anastasia, this is my Stella, " he said, in his deep voice. "You cannot see her plainly, but I tell you she is the sweetest little lady in the world, and you are to hasten to love each other as much as I love you both. "

Then in the half dark Stella stepped down and found herself embraced by a tall woman, while a voice as deep for a feminine one as Count Roumovski's was for a man whispered kind, nice things in the fluent English which brother and sister both used. And a feeling of warmth and security and happiness came over the poor child, to be in a haven of rest at last.

"Now we shall all pack in and get to Rome before dawn, " the princess said. "Sasha assures me the automobile will be faster than the train. "

So it was arranged, and, with Stella between them, the two Russians sat in the commodious back seat, and this time Count Roumovski allowed himself to encircle his beloved with his arm— and very often surreptitiously kissed her little ear and that delicious little curl of hair in her neck. She had taken off her hat, that its brim might not hit the princess, and had only the soft veil wound round her head, which loosened itself conveniently. This drive back to Rome was a time of pure enchantment to them both. And when the first streaks of dawn were coloring the sky they arrived at the door of the Excelsior Hotel, where Ivan had supper ordered and awaiting them.

The princess proved to be a handsome woman when they got into the light, with the same short face and wide eyes as her brother. Stella and she made immediate friends, and before they parted to try and sleep the princess said:

"Stella, that my brother loves you proves that you must be a very dear girl, that is what made me come from Paris at his instantaneous bidding. He is the most splendid character in the world, only don't cross his wishes. You will find it is no use, for one thing, " and she laughed her deep laugh. "He always knows best. "

"I am sure he does, " said Stella shyly. "I felt that at once, and so I did not hesitate. "

Next morning, when the three were seated at a merry early breakfast in the sitting-room discussing what should be said in Stella's letter to her Aunt Caroline, a loud knock came to the door, and, without waiting for a response, Canon Ebley and Stella's cousin, Mr. Deanwood, entered the room.

The princess rose with dignity, draping her silk morning wrapper round her like a statue, and Stella stepped forward with outstretched hand.

"Oh, Uncle Erasmus, " she said gaily, before any of the party could speak, "I am so glad to see you. I was just going to write to Aunt Caroline to tell her where I am, quite safe, in case she was worried about me. Let me introduce you to my future sister-in-law, Princess Urazov, with whom I am staying. My fiance, Count Roumovski, you have met before. "

Afterwards she often wondered how this emancipated spirit of daring had ever come to her. But she felt so joyous, so full of love and happiness, that it seemed that she could not be afraid or annoyed with anyone in the world.

"Stella, you are a shameless girl, " Canon Ebley retorted in a horrified voice. "I refuse to admit that you are engaged to this gentleman. Your whole conduct has been a scandalous series of deceptions and you must be ready to return at once with your aunt and your affianced husband. They are following us here now. "

Then Stella used a weapon that she had more than once found effectual with her uncle. She flung herself into his arms and clasped him round the neck. He was a short, portly man, and from this position she began to cajole him—while Count Roumovski looked on with amused calm, and his sister, following his lead, remained unmoved also.

Mr. Deanwood was the only restless person; he felt thoroughly uncomfortable and bored to death. He hated having been dragged into this family quarrel, and secretly sympathized with his cousin in her revolt at the thought of being Eustace Medlicott's wife.

"Oh, dear Uncle Erasmus! " Stella purred, from the highly perturbed clergyman's neck, where she was burrowing her sweet head, rubbing her peach-like cheek against his whiskered cheek. "Don't say those dreadful things, I have not deceived anybody, I have known Count Roumovski since the day after we came to Rome, and—and—I love him very much, and you know I always thought Eustace a bore, and you must agree it is wicked to marry and not to love, so it must be good to, oh! —well, to marry the person you do love. What have you to say against it? "

Canon Ebley tried to unclasp her arms from round his neck. He was terribly upset. To be sure, the girl was very dear to him, and had always been so sweet a niece, a truthful, obedient child from early infancy. Caroline had perhaps been a little hard—he had better hear the facts.

"Dear me, dear me, " he blurted out. "Well, well, tell me everything about the case, and, though I cannot consent to anything, I must do you the justice of hearing your side. "

"Won't you sit down here, sir? " Princess Urazov said, "and let my brother and your niece tell you their story. Mr. Deanwood, we met at Buda-Pesth two years ago—" and she turned to the young man and indicated that he should join her in the far window embrasure, which he did with alacrity, and from there they heard, interpolated in their personal conversation, scraps of the arguments going on between the three.

Stella, assisted by her lover, told of her first talk and her drive, and their rapidly ripening affection for each other, and the girl looked so happy and so pleading. Then Count Roumovski took up the thread. He explained his position, and how his view of life had always been direct in its endeavor to see the truth and the meaning of things, and how to him love was the only possible reason in ethical morality for any marriage between two people.

"It is merely a great degradation, otherwise, sir, " he said earnestly.

But here Canon Ebley was heard to protest that he could not understand a love which had sprung into being with such violence in the space of three days, and he felt very suspicious of its durability.

"Oh, Uncle Erasmus, how can you say that! " Stella interrupted him. "Why, you have often said that you yourself fell in love with Aunt Caroline from the moment your eye lighted upon her in church—in church, remember, you old darling! " and she nestled up against his shoulder again. Caresses like these she was always obliged to suppress in her austere aunt's presence; they were only to be indulged in upon great occasions, and to gain an important end, she knew! So the rogue smiled archly as she went on. "You could hardly wait until you were introduced at the garden party the next day, and Aunt Caroline said you proposed to her before the end of the week! "

"Come, come, " the cornered uncle growled, bridling, but a smile grew in his kindly eyes.

"There! " exclaimed Miss Rawson, triumphantly. "You cannot have another thing to say, except that you consent and wish us happiness. "

"It is true you are of age, Stella, " Canon Ebley allowed, "and if you like to take the law into your own hands, we cannot legally prevent you, as I have tried to explain this morning to your aunt and Eustace, but it is all very shocking and unusual, and very disturbing. You must remember, Count Roumovski is a foreigner, and we English people are prejudiced. I—fear for your happiness, my dear child! "

"You do not pay me a high compliment, sir, " Count Roumovski said, but without resentment. "Time, however, will prove whether I can take care of your niece or no. Do you feel any fear for yourself, Stella? "

"Not in the least, " Miss Rawson said, and they clasped fond hands. "I would go away with you, Sasha, to the ends of the earth now at once, and never ask you a single question. And I should certainly die if I were forced to go back to Eustace Medlicott. "

"Then I suppose there is nothing more to be said, " Canon Ebley stammered, upon which Stella again flung herself into his arms.

"Indeed, sir—I give you my word that you will not regret this decision, " Count Roumovski said gravely. "I believe your niece and I were made for one another. "

"We will hope so, " returned Canon Ebley, who could no longer keep up a stern resistance in the face of perfectly logical arguments and a witch of a girl purring over him and patting his cheek. He would have given in with a fair grace but for the awful knowledge that his stern spouse and the irate late fiance would arrive at any moment, and reproach him for his want of strength.

At this juncture of the affair, Princess Urazov came forward, and said with a gracious smile:

"Now I think you and I should agree with each other, sir; I had just as great cause for surprise as you had at the news of my brother's engagement to your niece, but I know and love him so well that I did not question the wisdom of his choice. And as you know and love your niece, can we not agree to try and make them happy together by giving them our blessing? After all, it is no crime for two young people to love each other! " and she put out her hands, which Canon Ebley, who was, after all, longing for peace, was obliged to take. Then with a charm and dignity that he was forced to admire, she drew him to the pair and placed his hand on their clasped hands, and her own over it.

"See, " she said, "Sasha and Stella, we both wish you all happiness and joy—is it not so? "

And Canon Ebley was constrained to murmur, "Yes. "

At this instant the door was opened violently, and the Aunt Caroline followed by the Reverend Eustace Medlicott burst into the room, brushing aside the frightened waiter, who would have prevented them; then they stopped dead short, petrified with astonishment,

78

and before she could prevent herself, Stella had pealed a silvery laugh, while she rushed forward and affectionately kissed her aunt.

"Dear Aunt Caroline, " she said. "Uncle Erasmus understands quite, and has given us his blessing, so won't you, too? "

But Mrs. Ebley was made of sterner stuff—she was horribly shocked, her feelings had been bruised in their tenderest parts, the laws of convention had been ruthlessly broken by her niece, and forgiveness was not for her.

She drew herself up with disgusted hauteur, while the Rev. Mr. Medlicott stood there glaring at the party too speechless with humiliation and pain to utter a word.

"Erasmus, " Mrs. Ebley said with scathing contempt. "I do not know how you have let yourself countenance this disgraceful scene, but I shall not do so. And if my niece still persists in bringing shame upon us all I must beg you to conduct me back to our hotel— I wash my hands of her and shall no longer own her as my sister's child, come"

At this, Stella gave a pitiful little cry and turned tender, beseeching eyes to her lover, and the sound of her voice touched that chord which was fine in Eustace Medlicott's heart. He seemed suddenly to see things as they were, and to realize that love had indeed come to his betrothed, though not for him, so he rose above the pain this conviction caused him and let justice have sway.

He strode forward and joined the group.

"You must not say that, Mrs. Ebley, " he said, "since your husband seems satisfied, there must have been some proper explanation made. You should hear them first. But I, for my part, wish to state now, in the presence of everyone, that if Miss Rawson can assure me she has made this choice of her own free will, and because she loves this gentleman—" here there was a break in the tones—"I can have nothing further to say and will give her back her freedom and make my retreat. "

"Oh, Eustace, thank you, " said Stella, gratefully holding out her hand. "I knew I could eventually count upon your goodness. I do indeed love Count Roumovski, and why should not we all be happy

79